ROAD
TO
JUSTICE

16-10-22

A Mountain Mystery

Meg,
Welcome back to Olde Bear
Hope you enjoy Jack Fowler's
latest case.

D.R.
Dom

SHOULTZ

2

Author's Note

This is a work of fiction. Names, characters, places, and incidents are the product of the author's imagination or are used fictitiously, and any resemblance to actual persons, living or dead, business establishments, events or locales is entirely coincidental.

Notice to Readers

Road to Justice is a sequel to **Butcher Road**, featuring Jack Fowler, the strong, silent Army veteran turned small-town detective. In both novels, the no-nonsense detective seeks clues to grisly crimes haunting the town of Stonefield, North Carolina.

While this sequel stands on its own, there are spoilers to **Butcher Road** included. If you intend to read both mysteries, it is suggested that you read them in sequence.

Look for Jack Fowler to appear in future Mountain Mysteries.

Also by D.R. Shoultz

Mountain Mystery Series
At the River's Edge
Butcher Road
Fallen from Sight
A Town Divided
A Town in Fear
Dark River
Road to Justice

Miles Stevens Series
Melting Sand
Cyber One
Gone Viral

Short Story Collections
It Goes On
Most Men

- DAY 1 -

Friday Night - Late September

"STONEFIELD EMS. What's your emergency?"

"This is Rand Elliott. My wife's been murdered. Get someone here now!"

"What's your location?" the dispatcher asked.

"I'm at Twenty-one Crescent Drive in Ridgeview Estates. I just got home and found my wife on our bedroom floor. She's been stabbed."

"Did you attempt CPR?"

"She's dead!" Elliott bellowed. "Get the police here now!"

"Officers will be there in a few minutes. Stay on the line until they arrive."

Dressed in a suit with his tie pulled loose, the tall, fair-haired businessman looked down at his wife of 16 years.

Sarah Elliott was faceup on the floor at the foot of their bed, her naked body partially covered by an open bathrobe. Blood had soaked the white robe and pooled on the carpet near her waist. A penetrating gash oozed blood from her chest, and her arms and hands had been slashed.

Elliott knelt beside his wife. Her blue eyes were fixed open, staring into nothingness. He caressed her face, cupping his hand against her smooth porcelain cheek. Sarah's skin was cool and clammy, her short blonde hair tangled. A clean, damp towel lay near her on the floor, possibly used to wrap her hair after stepping from the shower.

1

He slowly stood, blood staining the knees of his slacks.

Suddenly, blue and red lights strobed through the cracks of the bedroom shutters. He raised the phone back to his face.

"The police are here," he told the waiting dispatcher.

"Meet them at the door with your hands visible," she replied.

The 38-year-old Elliott stepped onto the porch as two vehicles skidded to the curb. Uniformed officers leapt from both sides of a black and gold Stonefield PD squad car. The younger of the two was slightly built with unruly dark hair. His partner was in his 40s with a bulldog face and beefy forearms. A third man wearing a blue blazer stepped from a vintage-looking grey sedan parked behind the police car. Near Elliott's age, the fit, dark-haired man with a square jaw led the uniformed officers to the front of the house.

As the three men reached the front porch, the one in the sport coat stepped forward and flashed his badge.

"I'm Detective Jack Fowler with Stonefield PD," he announced. "This is Officer Warren and Officer Sillar. Tell us what happened."

"My wife's in the bedroom. She's been murdered," Elliott replied, agony gripping his face and voice.

"Anyone else inside?" Fowler asked.

"No. We live alone. Whoever did this is gone."

"Take us to your wife."

The lawmen followed Elliott inside and down the hall toward the bedroom. Reaching open double doors, Fowler held up his hand, keeping the officers in the hallway.

Elliott paused with Fowler standing behind him. His eyes locked onto his dead wife as his lower lip trembled and his arms fell limp to his sides.

"I found her when I got home. There was nothing I could do."

Fowler had experienced gruesome crime scenes as a detective. While serving with Army Special Forces overseas, he'd seen firsthand what the horrors of war could do to the human body. But what he saw on the floor of the bedroom was different. This was a defenseless woman, stabbed to death in her own home, her arms and hands slashed to the bone.

The horrific scene triggered Fowler's PTSD. A chill came over his body, and he froze with his eyes fixed on the slain woman. Recognizing the symptoms, he took in a deep breath, released it slowly, and then took in another. The officers waited as the tension passed from Fowler's face.

"You okay?" Officer Warren asked.

"I'm fine," Fowler replied, brushing aside his concern.

Fowler stepped forward for a closer look, being careful to avoid the bloodstains. The cuts on the victim's arms and hands indicated that she'd fought to defend herself.

"How long ago did you find her?" he asked, moving back.

"It's been fifteen minutes. I'd just returned from work."

Fowler turned toward the two officers. "You guys check out the house and yard."

Warren and Sillar pulled their weapons and hurried down the hallway as Fowler turned his attention to the shaken man standing before him.

Blood soaked the knees of Elliott's pants and was smeared across the front of his shirt and his right coat sleeve. Fowler leaned closer to Elliott, looking for splatter spots or other telltale signs of a struggle.

"Can you explain the blood on your clothes?" he asked.

3

"As soon as I found her, I went to see what I could do," Elliott replied. "Blood was everywhere."

"What about that cut on the back of your right hand?" Fowler asked, staring at a 2-inch-long abrasion.

Elliott frowned, pulling his hand back.

"I scraped it on a stair banister this morning at my office. Why?"

Fowler continued to study the wound.

"Take me through what you did after finding your wife."

Elliott stared across the room with a far-off daze as he recalled his initial terror.

"Mr. Elliott, did you hear me?"

"Yeah. I heard you," he mumbled.

"Tell me what you did after finding your wife."

"I checked for her pulse and listened for her breaths, but she was gone," Elliott struggled to reply. "I took a minute to look through the house and then called nine-one-one. That was it."

"Did you disturb anything?" Fowler asked.

"Disturb?"

"Did you open or close doors or windows or move anything after coming home?"

"No. The house was dark and quiet when I arrived. I was concerned and immediately called for Sarah and found her here."

"Is anything missing?" Fowler continued.

"I'm not sure. I haven't checked. But other than Sarah's jewelry, we don't have many valuables in the house," Elliott replied. "Certainly nothing worth killing my wife."

"Show me where you keep the jewelry."

Elliott walked to the bedroom dresser and opened the top right drawer. He pushed aside his wife's underwear to reveal a wood panel with a hidden compartment below. He pried up the panel. A diamond necklace, tennis bracelet, and assorted rings sparkled inside, reflecting the light in the room.

"It's all here," he said, before replacing the panel and shutting the drawer.

"Did you see anyone or anything unusual as you drove up your street tonight?" Fowler asked.

"Nothing, but our street is dark. Trees have grown around the only streetlight."

"How well do you know your neighbors?"

"Not well. We're friends with Stan and Joan Felton around the corner," he replied, pointing a finger in the general direction. "We were supposed to have dinner with them at the club tonight, but I was late getting home."

"Is the street out front the only way to get to your house?" Fowler asked.

"It's the only road. The golf course runs along our backyard. I guess someone could follow the cart paths to get here."

The two officers returned to the bedroom.

"House is clear. No sign of anyone," the younger officer announced. "None of the doors or windows appeared to be forced."

"You guys wait for the coroner and the CSI team," Fowler told the officers. "Mr. Elliott, it'll take several hours for SBI Forensics to process your home. Why don't you ride with me down to the police station? You can have a cup of coffee while I ask you a few more questions."

"Questions? What questions?" Elliott asked.

"It's standard procedure," Fowler replied. "We'll need to get your statement. I'll return later and talk with your neighbors to see if they saw or heard anything."

"What about Sarah?" Elliott asked, shifting his eyes back to his wife's body.

"There's nothing you can do, Mr. Elliott," Fowler replied. "Before we go downtown, you should change your clothes and leave everything you're wearing on the floor of the bathroom, including your underwear. The forensic team will want to inspect it."

"Inspect it? What are you implying?" Elliott bristled.

"I'm not implying anything. You don't want to sit around the police station with blood all over your clothes."

Reluctantly, Rand went to his closet and grabbed a fresh shirt and pants before stepping into the bathroom and changing. The detective then led Elliott out the front of the house to his grey sedan.

Elliott sat in silence, staring forward from the passenger seat as Fowler started the car. Neither man said a word as the Chrysler sedan, once owned by Fowler's father, lumbered toward the front gate of Stonefield Estates. The Grey Ghost, as Fowler referred to his car, seemed to live up to its name as it escorted Rand Elliott from a nightmarish scene.

As they passed the stately two-story stone-clad clubhouse, a lone car was leaving the nearly vacant parking lot. Elliott glanced briefly in its direction, hoping no one saw him.

The news of Sarah's murder will spread quickly, he thought.

-1.1-

FOR THE MOST PART, Stonefield, North Carolina was a peaceful town on its way to becoming a city. Located between Charlotte to the south and the Blue Ridge Mountains to the northwest, Stonefield's 35,000 residents suffered from a split identity. Many, including families who had lived in Stonefield for generations, preferred the slow-paced lifestyle offered by the serenity of the mountains less than an hour away. On the other hand, newcomers flocked to Stonefield for its proximity to Charlotte, with access to higher-paying jobs and the attractions a big city could offer.

Jack Fowler grew up in one of Stonefield's middle-class neighborhoods, where he was an above average student and a three sports athlete at Stonefield Eastside High School. Following graduation, he enrolled in the law enforcement program at Piedmont Community College. Motivated by the September 11th attacks on the U.S., he enlisted in the Army after getting his associate's degree.

Fowler was promoted to the rank of sergeant in Army Special Forces while deployed to Afghanistan. He was injured in battle and returned to his hometown a decorated soldier and a changed man.

War had taken a toll on his body as well as his mind. Suffering from PTSD, it took years for Fowler to reacclimate to life back in Stonefield. His father, the former chief of the Stonefield Police Department (SPD), had suffered a fatal heart attack while Jack was overseas, adding to Fowler's mental strain and anxiety.

Bill Pierce, SPD's current Chief of Police, convinced Fowler to follow in his father's footsteps and join the force. It turned out to be the right move. Fowler's army experience and having grown up the son of a police officer made him a perfect fit for the role. While continuing to recover from the ill effects of war, Fowler focused on his police work. After an unusually short stint as a police officer, Fowler quickly became an asset to SPD's investigative unit.

More than a year earlier, a string of senseless murders had haunted the citizens of Stonefield and stressed the limited resources of the small-town police department. Prior to these killings, it had been three decades since the last Stonefield homicide, and SPD was ill-prepared for what it faced.

For no apparent reason, homeless men living in abandoned buildings along Butcher Road had been targeted by a serial killer. Fowler, a young detective on the force, was assigned to hunt down the murderer.

The Butcher Road investigations took a toll on Stonefield's police force. Before bringing the killer to justice, Chief Pierce had been badly wounded, and one of SPD's officers was murdered.

AS FOWLER DROVE back to the police station, he thought of the homeless drug addicts killed a year earlier. The murder of Sarah Elliott was different. She was from a prominent Stonefield family and neighborhood. While the burden felt by SPD to solve the Butcher Road killings was palpable, he expected the pressure on the department this time would be even more intense. Once the residents of Stonefield Estates learned of the brutal murder, they would demand that SPD bring the killer to justice.

As they approached the police station, Rand Elliott looked like a man hopelessly lost. Since leaving his home, he sat staring out the front car window, hands clasped on his lap, his face a blank canvas.

What Fowler observed at the crime scene made him believe Elliott was innocent, but his training and experience taught him not to jump to conclusions.

His discussion with Elliott wouldn't be easy. Fowler, too, had experienced the tragic and sudden loss of those close to him—on the battlefield and at home. He couldn't let the empathy he felt for Elliott get in the way of doing his job.

Fowler coasted his cruiser to the front of the police station and parked at a reserved spot just outside the entrance. The detective led Elliott up the steps and through the lobby to an empty conference room adjacent to Chief Pierce's office.

"Have a seat," Fowler said. "I need a couple of minutes with the chief. Can I get you anything to drink?"

"Just some water," Elliott replied.

Fowler retrieved a bottle of water from the break room down the hall before stepping next door to Chief Bill Pierce's office. The door was cracked open, so he pushed it aside and stepped in.

Hearing the door hinge squeal, Pierce snapped his head up from reading a report. The beefy man with close-cropped grey hair was perched behind a large oak desk. He was dressed in a snug khaki uniform adorned with official SPD patches; a gold badge stuck to his barrel chest.

"What did you find out?" Pierce asked.

"Rand Elliott, husband of the victim, says he arrived home after work and discovered his wife dead on the floor of their bedroom," Fowler began. "She'd been stabbed in the chest, with deep lacerations on her hands and arms."

"How's the husband doing?"

"He's not saying much, but he's cooperating. There were no signs of forced entry, and he claims he didn't see anyone or anything when he arrived."

"Do you think he's involved?" Pierce asked.

"I'm not sure, but I don't believe so. He seems to be in shock. He does have a scrape on his right hand that he claims he got at work."

"Could this be a burglary gone bad?"

"So far, it appears nothing's been taken," Fowler replied.

"Have you run a background check on this Elliott? Maybe he has some skeletons in his closet."

"No, not yet, but I brought him in for questioning. I better get back in there and get started."

"Have Jenkins sit in with you," Pierce said. "I want him to partner with you on this case."

Fowler grimaced.

"Seriously? Jenkins?"

"We're gonna get a lot of focus on this murder, and I want to show that we're assigning our most experienced team to the case."

"Jenkins may be the senior detective on the force, but he's never worked a murder case. Hell, he was working carjackings during the Butcher Road murders."

"It's where he was needed at the time," Pierce shot back.

"The SBI is likely to assign someone to this investigation," Fowler replied. "Why not request Angela Jones? She's more than proven herself."

"I'm aware of your high regard for Detective Jones," Pierce said, locking eyes with his young detective.

Fowler tensed.

"My request isn't personal. She'd clearly be a better resource than Jenkins."

"Her availability is up to the SBI. For now, I want you and Jenkins to run with this," Pierce insisted.

Fowler thinned his lips and shook his head. "Where's Jenkins now?" he asked. "We can't keep Elliott waiting forever."

"I called him at home. He's been at his desk on the computer, looking for information on the Elliotts."

"I assume I have the lead on this case," Fowler said, his comment not sounding like a question.

"Yeah," Pierce replied. "But consider this an opportunity to work on your teamwork. There are ways for you to lead without issuing orders. SPD isn't Army Special Forces."

Fowler accepted the chief's advice and headed out the door to find Jenkins.

A tall, clean-shaven detective dressed in a white shirt and narrow dark tie that draped to his belt approached from the other end of the corridor. The 60-year-old lawman was one of only two men on the police force to serve longer than Fowler's father. The other was Chief Pierce.

Jenkins nodded and cracked a smile as he approached. Fowler's expression remained stoic. He waited at the door to the conference room for the distinguished-looking man with silver temples to arrive.

Brooks Jenkins had served twenty years as a uniformed officer in SPD before Jack Fowler, Sr. promoted him to detective. The only black police officer in the department at the time, Jenkins had earned the respect of the community he served as well as the respect of Jack's father. This would be the first case Jenkins and Fowler worked together.

"It took nearly thirty years, but it appears I've finally landed a murder case," Jenkins said.

"I look forward to working with you," Fowler replied unconvincingly.

"You brought in the husband?" Jenkins asked.

"Yeah. He's pretty shaken. He didn't say anything on the drive to the station. If you don't mind, I'd like to take the lead on the questions."

"Sure," Jenkins replied. "Not a problem."

They both knew Chief Pierce had set the ground rules for the investigation, with Fowler taking the lead, but neither would broach the subject.

"Pierce said you were doing a background check on Elliott and his wife."

"I didn't find much," Jenkins replied. "Rand Elliott has a clean record. Not even a traffic ticket. His wife, Sarah, was charged with a DUI five years ago. It was her only offense, so she paid a minimal fine and that was it."

"What about occupations?"

"Elliott works for Biogen Technologies in Charlotte. His title is director of marketing. I'm not sure what he sells. The company website was way over my head."

"And the victim?"

"She was a criminal defense attorney. As best I can tell, she was a one-woman firm, sharing downtown office space with another attorney. Her Facebook page makes her out to be a crusader for the wrongly accused."

"A criminal defense attorney?" Fowler asked, shaking his head. "I have a feeling this is going to get messy really quick. You find anything else?"

"No. That's about it."

Fowler opened the door and stepped inside with Detective Jenkins hovering over his shoulder. Elliott was slumped forward in a chair, clasping his hands between his knees. He glanced up at the detectives. His face was pale and emotionless.

"This is Detective Jenkins. He's been assigned to investigate this case and will sit in on our discussion."

Elliott's expression remained unchanged, briefly studying Jenkins and then looking back down at his clasped hands.

"Can I get you anything before we begin?" Fowler asked.

Elliott shook his head.

Fowler and Jenkins took seats across the table. The young detective pulled a small recorder from his coat pocket and placed it on the oval table between him and Elliott.

"This is easier than taking notes," he said, switching it on.

"I can't focus right now," Elliott said. "Can't this wait until tomorrow?"

"There's nowhere for you to go right now," Fowler replied, "other than a hotel. And we've found it's best to get statements as soon as possible while memories are fresh."

"I called my sister in Charlotte while I was waiting. She insisted I come stay with her."

"This won't be any easier tomorrow," Fowler said.

Elliott shifted nervously from side to side, staring at Fowler and then Jenkins.

"Go ahead," Elliott finally replied, "but make it quick."

They all took deep breaths, settling into their chairs.

"Do you have any idea who would do this to your wife? Has she ever been threatened or had arguments with anyone?" Fowler asked.

"She's a criminal defense attorney. Her life is dealing with tough people, many who disagree with her."

"Was she currently working any high-profile or dangerous cases?"

"We didn't discuss her work much. Few of her cases ever made the news," he replied before pausing. "She'd been working in Asheville off and on the past month or so. I think she was defending some punk accused of peddling drugs."

"Do you know the defendant's name?" Fowler asked.

"Not a clue, but I'm sure the case is on the county court docket."

Fowler turned to Jenkins.

"I'll follow up," the senior detective offered, jotting down a note.

"Has she mentioned any other cases?"

"No. Like I said, we didn't discuss her work much."

"You said your wife's been in Asheville the past month. Does she stay over or commute?"

"Depends on the case. Lately, she's been staying during the week, coming back on Fridays."

"Do you know where she stays?"

"I assume a downtown hotel near the courthouse," Elliott replied. "I don't arrange her itinerary."

"Does she work with anyone? A secretary or paralegal?"

"She usually works alone. If a case gets too big, contract lawyers sometimes assist."

"What attorneys have worked with her in the past?"

"She shares an office with Eldon Watkins, but I'm not sure if they actually share cases."

"Was your wife working in Asheville today?"

"Yeah. She told me she'd be home in time for dinner with our neighbors, the Feltons."

"Have you talked to the Feltons today?"

"No, I was running late, so I assume Sarah cancelled our plans."

Fowler paused as he considered his next question.

"Have you noticed anything out of the ordinary in your neighborhood recently? Any strangers, or anything out of place?"

"Not really," Elliott replied. "I don't get home until after sunset most days. Not much to notice in the dark."

"Tell me about your work," Fowler said.

"I work for a company that manufactures and sells high-tech equipment used to develop new pharmaceuticals."

"So, you sell to large pharmas?"

"Yeah. And to chemical companies. Pfizer, Dow, Merck, Abbott, and AbbVie to name a few."

"A lot of travel involved?"

"Sure, but not as much as in the past. Telecommuting has helped."

"Have you made any enemies recently, either customers or maybe competitors?" Fowler asked matter-of-factly.

Elliott's head snapped back.

"Are you asking if I've pissed someone off enough for them to cut up my wife? I work in a highly competitive business, but it's *all* business. It's not personal."

Fowler glanced toward Jenkins. The senior detective frowned before looking away.

"Is it correct to assume that you have no idea who might've had a motive to do harm to your wife?"

"Did you see my wife? Did you?" Elliott asked, his voice cracking. "I can't imagine anyone having a motive to do *that* to another human being. And if I did, you can bet your ass I wouldn't be here wasting my time with you. I'd be hunting them down."

Elliott rose to his feet and wiped his face with the palm of his hand.

"Now, if you don't mind, my sister is waiting to hear from me."

-1.2-

FOWLER AND JENKINS escorted Rand Elliott out of the police station to Fowler's sedan. With Elliott seated in the back, they exited the parking lot and drove four miles in silence to Stonefield Estates.

It was approaching midnight when Elliott was allowed to enter his home. Under the watchful eye of Officer Warren, he stepped to his bedroom to retrieve supplies for an overnight stay at his sister's. His wife's body had been removed, but her bloodstains greeted him on the carpet. The site made him dizzy. For a moment, he bent over, hands on his knees, choking back tears.

He finally stood and plodded slowly toward the bathroom and then to his closet, placing several items in a small overnight bag.

Elliott hadn't had time to charge his Tesla after returning home, so he placed the suitcase on the passenger seat of his wife's black Range Rover and stepped behind the wheel. With Fowler and Jenkins watching from the driveway, Elliott backed out of the garage and drove away without looking back.

After several hours of searching the home, the two-person forensic team loaded supplies into the rear of a white van parked at the far end of the house. Officers Warren and Sillar had also been on site the whole time. They approached Fowler and Jenkins as they stood in the driveway.

"I just spoke with Inspector Williams. I don't think they found much," the stocky Warren told the detectives.

"No murder weapon?" Fowler asked.

"No, and no fingerprints in the bedroom other than the victim and her husband," Warren replied.

"The killer was likely wearing gloves, but with all that blood, there had to be footprints," Fowler said.

"Other than the husband's, only your footprints were in the bedroom," Officer Warren said.

"I was careful where I stepped," Fowler replied defensively. "I'm sure I never tracked any blood."

"Bloodspots were tracked throughout the house. The initial assessment of the forensic team is the prints match the shoes Rand Elliott left in the bathroom before going with you to the station."

"How sure are they?"

"Very," the officer replied.

"What did the coroner say about time of death?" Detective Jenkins asked.

"Doc Richards said she'd been dead less than three hours but probably longer than an hour. His assessment is based on the blood not being completely dry and rigor mortis not yet present."

"Rand Elliott better hope someone saw him arrive home when he claims he did," Jenkins said.

"Have you talked to any of the neighbors?" Fowler asked the officers.

"I met a middle-aged couple out front who'd come to see what was going on, but I sent them home," Officer Sillar replied.

"Did you get their names?"

"Felton, I think. The man made a point of saying he was Dr. Felton. Didn't get the woman's name. They seemed rattled. The husband pressed me for information, but I didn't provide any."

Fowler glanced at his watch.

"It's too late to follow up with them now. We'll get the coroner's report early tomorrow and then call the forensic team. Let's plan on coming back out here in the morning and see what the neighbors can tell us."

- DAY 2 -

Saturday

FOWLER'S CELLPHONE chirped atop his dresser. It felt like it had only been minutes since he'd fallen asleep. He lowered his feet to the floor and sat for a moment before lumbering toward the irritating noise.

"It's six o'clock. Not everyone goes to bed at nine," Fowler greeted in a scratchy voice.

"Jack, I just heard about the murder!"

The slight Jamaican accent belonged to Detective Angela Jones with the North Carolina State Bureau of Investigation (SBI). The strong-willed, attractive detective served alongside Fowler in solving the Butcher Road murders a year earlier.

"That's right. The husband claims to have found his wife's body on their bedroom floor around nine last night. She'd been stabbed in the chest, with slashes on her arms and hands."

"Stabbings are an act of passion. She must've really pissed someone off."

"I didn't get home until a few hours ago, or I would've called."

"Do you think it was the husband?" Jones asked.

"Not sure, but if I had to guess, I'd say no."

"I'm betting whoever did it knows the woman," Jones said. "I assume you're working the investigation."

"Yeah. With Brooks Jenkins."

"Jenkins? I thought he was retiring. Why did Pierce assign him?"

"He wants an experienced team on this case. After Jessup retired a few months ago, Jenkins became his senior detective. I have to admit, Jenkins' salt and pepper hair does present an air of distinction."

"I'm glad he's giving Jenkins a shot at a big case," Jones said. "Pierce should be more proactive in promoting diversity on his force."

"Don't be so critical. Qualified applicants are hard to find in a small suburban town. Besides, Pierce and I have begged you to transfer to his detective unit."

"He'd love a Jamaican female on his team. But even if he made me a director, I doubt he could match my SBI salary."

"Okay. Enough about Pierce and your lofty salary. I assume you called because you're interested in getting involved with this case."

There was a pause on the line.

"I doubt that's gonna happen," she finally replied. "I was just appointed to lead a joint SBI and Charlotte-Mecklenburg PD team. We're looking into the rise in Charlotte's gang violence."

"You're serious?" Fowler asked. "I hope this isn't another study of the root causes driving inner-city youth to drugs and violence."

"You know my focus is getting the bad guys off the streets," Jones snapped.

"Come on, Angela. You're a crime detective, not a social worker. Let me talk to Pierce. I'm sure he'd be glad to make a call to get you on this investigation."

"It won't hurt me to spend some time understanding the makeup of inner-city gangs," Jones said. "Who knows? It might make me a better detective."

"So, you're gonna let me go this one alone?"

"You'll have Jenkins at your side," Jones replied. "And I'm sure we'll find time to get together."

"Speaking of getting together, I cancelled our trip for next weekend," Fowler said. "Sounds like it'll be a while before either of us gets any free time."

"How about a raincheck?"

"Sure," Fowler replied.

"And I've been known to make surprise visits," Jones teased.

She disconnected as Fowler was about to respond. He set the phone back on the dresser as his focus turned to the day ahead.

Stepping to the end of the bed, he pulled on the slacks he'd taken off only a few hours earlier. After washing his face and running a razor over his bristled beard, Fowler snatched a fresh dress shirt from his closet. He then slipped into his brown loafers and stepped down the hall to the kitchen.

As he waited for his coffee to brew, he stared out the window into the darkness of his backyard.

Angela's right, he thought. *This stabbing wasn't a random act. Whoever did this knew the victim.*

Fowler had arranged to meet Detective Jenkins at the police station at 7:30. Their first order of business was to get copies of the reports from the coroner and the forensic team and then head back out to Stonefield Estates to interview Rand Elliott's neighbors.

Fowler didn't feel like waiting until 7:30. As soon as the coffee finished brewing, he poured a cup into a travel mug, slipped on his holster and sport coat, and headed toward SPD headquarters.

THE SUN HAD YET TO RISE when Fowler's cruiser bounced over the curb and into the parking lot in front of the single-story brick building. News crews were waiting for him at the steps of the police station as he exited his car. Fowler paused, surveying the handful of reporters gathered. He approached them, holding his travel mug. The news crews had their microphones extended and cameras rolling.

The dark-haired, square-jawed, 36-year-old detective had become a familiar face to the local press during last year's murder investigations. He and Detective Jones were featured in multiple media reports. At first, the two were described as young, aggressive investigators, but after solving the case, the news stories took on a tabloid flair, focusing on their after-hours relationship.

"Detective Fowler, what can you tell us about the murder at Stonefield Estates last night?"

The question was posed by Jane Topper, an exuberant journalist from Charlotte's Channel 6. He recognized the toothy brunette from last year's press conferences during the Butcher Road investigations. She and two reporters from other news outlets stuck microphones into Fowler's face.

"I have nothing to say," Fowler replied, pushing the microphones aside and continuing toward the entrance. "I'm sure Chief Pierce will release a statement at the appropriate time."

The reporters continued bombarding him with questions:
"We understand a woman's been killed."
"Is this related to the Butcher Road murders?"
"Any suspects? Has anyone been charged?"

Fowler stepped through the glass doors, ignoring the peppering of questions as he passed.

From the lobby, he could see light seeping through the crack in the door to Chief Pierce's office. Fowler rapped lightly before sticking his head inside.

"Didn't take long for the vultures to circle, did it?" Fowler asked.

"I guess they're just doing their job," Pierce replied, shaking his head. "I came in the back entrance this morning."

"Did you hear anything from forensics or the coroner?" Fowler asked.

"Just got the coroner's report. Cause of death was a single puncture wound to the chest. It penetrated her heart," he replied, tossing the report onto the center of his desk.

"Evidence of a sexual assault?"

"No."

"What about time of death?"

"Best he could estimate was sometime between six and eight p.m. No murder weapon has been found, but the jagged cuts suggest a serrated blade. Maybe five to six inches in length."

"Anything back from SBI Forensics yet?"

As Fowler asked the question, Detective Jenkins entered the office.

"Check your email," Jenkins said. "The CSI report from Greensboro arrived ten minutes ago. I would have come down sooner, but I couldn't pull myself away. Looks like we need to bring the husband back in."

Pierce rotated his chair toward the computer and logged on. Jenkins and Fowler took positions over his shoulder.

"They discovered a knife in a trash bin at the street," Pierce announced.

"They must've found it after we left," Fowler said.

"Before they headed back to Greensboro, the inspectors decided to take a quick search of the trash bins set up and down the street for the next morning's collection," Jenkins said. "The knife was found two doors down, right on top of the garbage."

"Sounds pretty careless," Fowler said.

"Maybe whoever left it assumed the garbage pickup would come early," Pierce replied.

"Have they tested it?" Fowler asked, squinting as he attempted to read the report on the computer screen.

"The blood on the knife matches the victim," Jenkins said. "But that's not all. The prints on the handle match Rand Elliott."

Pierce pushed back from his desk and stood.

"Bring him in!"

"He's staying with his sister in Charlotte," Fowler replied. "She lives two hours away on the south side. Do you think we should have Charlotte-Mecklenburg PD make the arrest?"

Pierce thought for a moment.

"We've got a murder weapon with Elliott's prints. I'll get the warrant issued ASAP."

- 2.1 -

IT TOOK LESS THAN thirty minutes for CMPD to locate Rand Elliott at the home of Vickie and Reggie Swanson. Wearing dark helmets, visors, and protective vests, a six-man SWAT team pounded simultaneously at the front and back doors of the Swansons' residence.

"We have an arrest warrant for Rand Elliott for the murder of his wife!" the SWAT leader screamed through the front door. "Come out immediately!"

The Swansons leapt wide-eyed from the kitchen table where they were having a late breakfast with Elliott.

"What the hell's going on, Rand?" Reggie asked.

"It's a mistake. I talked to the detectives last night. They know I'm innocent."

"Apparently someone doesn't believe you," Reggie replied. "Get to the door before they knock it down."

Elliott hurried to the front door, swung it open, and began demanding answers, but the officers were in no mood to listen. Two of the heavily armed men pulled Elliott's arms behind him and slapped cuffs onto his wrists. A third officer read him his rights.

"This is bullshit! Where are you taking me?" Elliott screamed.

"Stonefield Police Department. You'll be held at the city jail until your arraignment."

"Call Eldon Watkins," Elliott shouted to his sister over his shoulder. "Tell him I've been arrested."

Vickie Swanson stood crying on her front porch as she watched the blue and white CMPD police car pull away with her brother staring through the back window.

AS THE PATROL CAR sped down I-77 with Rand Elliott in the back seat, attorney Eldon Watkins arrived at Stonefield's police station.

The tall, wiry, 68-year-old defense attorney looked like he'd just stepped out of the 1960s. Round, wire-rimmed glasses were perched on the narrow nose of his John Lennon-like face. His mostly grey hair was parted down the middle and pulled back into a stringy ponytail that draped a couple of inches over his shirt collar. He wore dark brown slacks and a tweed sport coat with leather patches on the elbows. It was not clear whether the unmatched vest actually came with the ensemble or was borrowed from a three-piece suit that had gone out of style decades ago. In lieu of a briefcase, a drab green canvas backpack was slung over his right shoulder.

"I'm here to see my client," he announced loudly, slapping his backpack onto the reception desk.

"Yes, sir. And who would that be?" the young officer behind the desk asked.

"Rand Elliott. I was told he was being held at the city jail."

Detectives Fowler and Jenkins were in the conference room next to Chief Pierce's office. They'd just gathered to map out the next steps in their investigation. The sound of the backpack smacking the desk along with Watkins' booming voice prompted Fowler to step to the open door.

"Elliott hasn't arrived yet," Fowler called to the visitor leaning on the desk. "Can I help you?"

"That depends on who you are," Watkins replied, picking up his backpack and turning toward the man in the doorway.

"I'm Detective Jack Fowler. And you are?"

"Eldon Watkins, the attorney representing Rand Elliott. I was asked to meet him here."

"Elliott is on his way from Charlotte. Should be here shortly."

"I need to see his arrest warrant," Watkins demanded.

"I'm sure that can be arranged once it's clear you're representing Mr. Elliott," Fowler replied calmly.

Watkins' narrow face wrinkled, annoyed by Fowler's response.

Jenkins stepped from the conference room, joining Fowler outside the doorway.

"This is my partner, Detective Jenkins," Fowler said. "Mr. Watkins here says he's representing Rand Elliott."

Jenkins nodded.

Watkins glanced briefly at the tall detective and then turned back to Fowler.

"I'll need to meet with Mr. Elliott as soon as he arrives. Any questioning of my client will be done in my presence."

"It should take only a few minutes to process his paperwork," Fowler said, remaining unfazed by Watkins' demands. "After that, I'd be glad to arrange for you to meet with him in the interrogation room down the hall."

"I know where it is," Watkins scoffed. "If you don't mind, I'll wait there."

The hippie-looking lawyer turned and strode down the hallway, disappearing into the room.

28

"I'm surprised he didn't remember me," Jenkins said. "I arrested one of his clients about six years ago."

"Really? Who was that?" Fowler asked.

"Can't remember the guy's name. He was a two-bit drifter pushing marijuana to teenagers in the mall parking lot north of town. Store owners alerted me to what was going on, and I picked him up."

"And *this* guy is who Elliott hired to defend him on a murder charge?"

"I did some checking on Watkins back then before the court appearance," Jenkins replied. "At one time, he had a reputation for successfully defending high-profile cases. He was a partner at a firm in Charleston, West Virginia in the late nineties."

"What brought him here?"

"It appeared he got sideways with the wrong people back in Charleston. Representatives from a steelworkers' union sued him and his law firm for defamation and won a multimillion-dollar settlement that ended up with Watkins leaving the firm."

"That still doesn't explain his connection to Rand Elliott."

"Watkins shares, or should I say shared, a downtown law office with Elliott's wife."

"You're not serious! I've lived here most of my life, and I've never noticed his office," Fowler said, furrowing his brow.

"It's not easy to spot," Jenkins replied. "It's at the corner of Main and Fifth above Smith's Sporting Goods."

"Was Elliott's wife practicing law with Watkins?"

"I don't think so. At least his website doesn't read that way."

"We'll need to find out what their connection was," Fowler said. "There's gotta be more to that story."

MOMENTS LATER, an angry Rand Elliott was led in handcuffs into the Stonefield Police Station by two husky Charlotte-Mecklenburg police officers still in dark SWAT uniforms. The commotion brought Detectives Fowler and Jenkins out of the conference room.

Elliott's face was red, his blond hair askew, and rings of sweat formed beneath his armpits.

"What the hell's going on?" Elliott shouted at Fowler. "You know damn well I didn't kill my wife!"

The young detective stared back through steel blue eyes.

"Take him to the jailer. He's waiting through that door," Fowler replied, pointing down the corridor to the entrance of the city jail located at the rear of the police station.

As the officers escorted Elliott down the hall and past the interrogation room, Watkins appeared in the doorway.

"Get me outta here," Elliott ordered his attorney. "You know I'd never do this."

"We'll talk soon."

It was all Watkins had time to say before Elliott disappeared behind the jailhouse door.

- 2.2 -

AFTER REVIEWING THE ARREST WARRANT and the charges filed against his client by the DA's office, Watkins was permitted to meet with Rand Elliott.

Wearing an orange jumpsuit and handcuffs, Elliott shuffled into the ten-by-ten-foot interrogation room led by a lanky jailer in a khaki uniform. The prisoner flopped into a seat across from Watkins at a small metal table.

"I'll be outside," the jailer said as he stepped into the hall and shut the door.

"What's going on, Rand?" Watkins asked, leaning forward. "I talked to Sarah earlier in the week. Everything seemed fine."

"This is bullshit! Get me outta here."

"It's not gonna be that easy. The DA is requesting bail be set at one million."

"That's ridiculous! Of all people, you should know that I didn't kill Sarah."

"Setting your bail isn't up to me. The DA has evidence to support the charges," Watkins replied.

"What evidence?"

"They found a knife with your prints in a trash can down the street. The blood on the knife matches Sarah's."

Elliott froze, locking eyes with Watkins. You could almost hear the wheels spinning inside Elliott's head.

"You need to level with me, Rand. Are you responsible for Sarah's death?"

"Absolutely not! I found her body when I got home around nine o'clock," Elliott replied defiantly. "I didn't kill her, and I have no idea who did."

"Right now, it doesn't look good. They have a murder weapon with your prints and no evidence that anyone else had entered your home."

Elliott slumped forward and blew out a long breath.

"This isn't happening. I swear I didn't kill Sarah! You gotta believe me."

"The one thing they're missing is a motive," Watkins said. "Please tell me they won't find one."

"I had no reason to kill my wife."

"Tell me about your relationship."

"You knew Sarah. We both were workaholics. We saw each other mainly on weekends. What else do you need to know?"

"Any recent disagreements?"

"Sure, but none were motives for murder. Same ol' stuff. All work and no play. You know how it is."

"You're gonna get drilled on your alibi. Can you prove you weren't home between six and eight?"

"I was in Charlotte. I called Sarah around five-thirty to cancel our dinner plans."

"Where were you from five-thirty to nine?"

Guilt spread across Elliott's face.

"I lied to Sarah. I told her my meeting was running long. Instead, I made plans to meet a client for a drink around six-thirty, but she didn't show. I had a couple drinks while I watched a ballgame and left at seven-thirty, maybe a little later."

"She?" Watkins asked, his eyes widening.

"It was about business. Beth Adams is the head of development at Delco Pharma. You can check her out if you want."

"Can anyone place you at the bar?"

"It's called Fool's Gold, near the four eighty-five exit. I've been there a few times, but I doubt anyone would remember me."

"Did you pay with a credit card?"

"No. I threw down thirty bucks and left."

Watkins sighed as he pulled his hand back over his slicked-back hair.

"Did you use your cellphone prior to arriving at your home?"

"I received a call from Beth shortly after getting to the bar, cancelling our plans. I guess it was around six-fifteen or so. After that, I powered off my phone."

"Powered it off? Why?"

"The only calls I'd get late on a Friday would be from my wife or my boss. At the time, I didn't want either."

Watkins shook his head in disbelief.

"Let's hope someone at the bar remembers you, or one of your neighbors saw you arrive home."

A knock at the door was followed by Detectives Fowler and Jenkins stepping inside.

"Your time is up," Fowler said, shutting the door and pulling out a chair at the table. "We've got a few questions for Mr. Elliott."

Fowler moved his chair closer to the prisoner and sat while Jenkins remained standing near the door.

"Let's start with telling us where you were immediately prior to arriving home."

Elliott turned to Watkins, looking for guidance.

"My client has informed me he was on his way home from a business meeting in Charlotte. He stopped to meet with a client for a drink around six-thirty. His client had a change of plans so he had a couple drinks alone and drove home, arriving around nine p.m."

"And someone can verify your whereabouts?" Fowler asked.

"I talked to my client around six-fifteen, maybe a little later," Elliott quickly replied. "She can confirm our plans. I'm sure the call and my location at that time can be verified."

"That still leaves nearly three hours unaccounted for," Fowler said. "If you had a cellphone, we should be able to verify your location."

"I turned off my phone after talking to my client. Any calls late on a Friday are usually bad news. I make a habit of turning it off after six or so."

"You expect me to believe that?" Fowler scowled. "Sounds more like you didn't want anyone to know where you were."

"Let's not jump to conclusions," Watkins interrupted loudly. "I'll get you the name of the establishment and phone number of the client who cancelled. You can take it from there. I'm sure you'll be able to verify Mr. Elliott's accounting of his time."

Fowler paused.

"How would you describe your relationship with your wife?"

"Detective, my client has nothing else to say today. I suggest you broaden your search for suspects," Watkins said defiantly. "Ms. Elliott was a defense attorney, and she worked for and against people with checkered pasts. Mr. Elliott had no motive for killing his wife. Maybe you can find someone else who did."

"You sound like you may have someone in mind," Fowler said, turning to Watkins.

"Not really," he replied. "But I suggest you start with her most recent cases."

"And *I* suggest you work on an alibi for your client," Fowler rebutted. "As of now, the DA has sufficient evidence to charge Mr. Elliott with the murder of his wife. We'll continue to investigate, but at this time, we aren't looking for *other* suspects."

"Then we're done for today," Watkins replied.

Fowler pushed his chair from the table and rose as Detective Jenkins opened the door.

"Jailer!" Fowler called. "Take the prisoner back to his cell."

- 2.3 -

WITH FOWLER BEHIND THE WHEEL, he and Detective Jenkins headed toward Stonefield Estates. Fall was making an early appearance in the North Carolina town. There was a chill in the air, and the trees cascading up the hillsides were already showing signs of a colorful autumn.

"Don't you think it's time you spring for new wheels?" Jenkins asked, glancing around the inside of the vintage sedan.

"I've always had an affinity for vintage vehicles. On the rare occasions I get free time, I work on restoring my Jeep Wagoneer. I've had it since high school."

"I could understand you driving a Jeep, but this lump of iron doesn't exactly fit the image of a successful, young detective."

"To the contrary," Fowler smirked. "The Grey Ghost perfectly fits my image. It's experienced a few setbacks, shows signs of wear, but it's dependable and gets the job done."

"And I'm sure it impresses the ladies," Jenkins said, smiling.

"I only have one lady I need to impress, and she doesn't seem to mind my taste in cars."

"What do you think we're gonna hear from Elliott's neighbors?" Jenkins asked.

"I don't know what to expect, but I hope someone saw him arrive home Friday night," Fowler replied.

"You think he's guilty?"

"I'm not sure."

Jenkins tilted his head and raised an eyebrow.

"Even with his fingerprints on the murder weapon?" he asked.

"There's a lot that doesn't add up just yet," Fowler replied.

"How so?"

"First of all, Elliott was wearing a suit when we arrived. Who kills his wife with a knife wearing a business suit and doesn't even bother to hide the blood stains?"

"What about the cut on his hand and the murder weapon with his prints?" Jenkins asked.

"I looked closely at the cut. It was more of an abrasion and had already scabbed."

"And the knife?"

"If you had just stabbed your wife to death, would you risk running out to the curb with blood all over your clothes and stashing the knife where someone could possibly find it, and then run back into the house?"

"Well, *someone* put it there," Jenkins replied. "And once the trash was picked up the next morning, no one would've ever found it."

"Maybe it *was* Elliott who put it there. But it just seems too staged for me."

"Fingerprints don't lie."

"True. The prints are hard to explain away," Fowler admitted.

The grey sedan passed through the entrance of the upscale neighborhood and wound its way around the curbed streets to the home of Joan and Dr. Stan Felton.

A lawn maintenance crew was making a late-season pass over the Feltons' yard, sucking leaves from around the shrubs.

Dressed in blue sport coats and creased slacks, the detectives stepped to the front porch of the sprawling ranch. Fowler rang the doorbell.

An attractive brunette in her early fifties, trying to look thirty, opened the door dressed in skinny jeans and a red sweater. She scanned the men on her porch from head to toe.

"You gentlemen look like cops," she said "What's going on over at the Elliotts?"

"Are you Mrs. Felton?" Fowler asked.

She nodded.

"I'm Detective Fowler, and this is my partner, Detective Jenkins. Do you have time to answer some questions?"

"Fowler?" she blurted, eyes widening. "You're the one who solved the Butcher Road murders with that cute black cop."

"Yes, that's right," he replied curtly. "If you don't mind, we have a few questions for you this morning. May we step inside? It's a little noisy out here."

"Sure. Forgive me," she said, opening the door and directing them into the wide foyer. "I guess I'm still rattled from all the commotion last night."

"I understand you talked to police officers in front of the Elliotts' home," Fowler began.

"Yes, Stan and I were supposed to have dinner with Sarah and Rand, but they canceled. After returning home, we saw the police cars and lights at their house, so we walked over."

A dark-haired man with silver temples, square jaw, and no-nonsense expression stepped up the hallway from the back of the home. He was wearing a blue jogging suit with a white towel draped around his neck. He pulled back his shoulders and sucked in his gut as he approached.

"This is my husband, Stan," she said. "This is Detective Fowler and Detective Jenkins."

"Dr. Felton," he said, nodding to the two men. "Forgive my appearance. I just returned from a run. It's my five-mile day."

He wiped his forehead with the towel and adjusted his snug jogging suit.

"Impressive," Fowler replied. "We stopped by to ask you and your wife a few questions this morning. And if you don't mind, Detective Jenkins will be taking notes."

"Fine with me," he replied. "Is this about the Elliotts? I heard on the news this morning that Sarah's dead and Rand's in jail."

"Unfortunately, that's true. Detective Jenkins and I have been assigned to investigate her murder."

"You recognize Detective Fowler, don't you, Stan?" Mrs. Felton asked. "He was the one who solved those awful killings last year."

"Yeah. He looks familiar," her husband replied, unimpressed. "Let's give him a chance to ask his questions."

"Did you happen to see Rand Elliott arrive home Friday night?" Fowler asked.

"No. We were at the clubhouse having dinner until nine or so," Mrs. Felton replied. "Like I said before, we saw the police lights shortly after getting home. After a while, our curiosity got the best of us, so we walked over to see what was going on."

"When was the last time you talked to either of the Elliotts?" Fowler asked.

"Sarah called me before six on Friday to say Rand was running late, and we should go ahead without them."

"How did she sound?"

"Fine. Just a little disappointed about cancelling, I guess."

"It's not as though their cancelling was anything new," Dr. Felton scoffed. "I'm not sure Rand has ever been on time."

"How would you describe the Elliotts' relationship? Have you ever witnessed any tension or disputes?" Fowler asked.

"They seemed to get along fine," Mrs. Felton replied. "They're very busy people, but I had the impression they enjoyed doing things together."

"Come on, Joan. Let's not give these detectives the wrong impression," Dr. Felton huffed. "That marriage cooled off years ago. The last time we went out with them, Sarah never said two words. You could've cut the air with a knife."

Fowler winced at the bad choice of words.

"What was the source of their tension?" Jenkins asked, continuing to take notes.

"Rand is a young, good-looking man. I haven't seen him with other women, but he gave off that vibe, if you know what I mean," Dr. Felton replied.

"Stan, you're speculating and spreading rumors," his wife argued.

"Maybe. Maybe not. All I can say is he seemed to always be the reason Sarah had to cancel their plans."

Fowler glanced at Jenkins.

"What about Mrs. Elliott? Do either of you know if she was concerned about her safety, or if she ever mentioned any disagreements or arguments with anyone?" Fowler asked.

Mrs. Felton placed a finger to her chin and thought for a moment.

"I was as close to her as anyone in this neighborhood, and she never mentioned anything to me. Even in her line of work, there wasn't much that scared her," she replied.

"She never mentioned anything to me, either," her husband added. "But I rarely spoke to her without Rand present."

Detective Fowler handed Dr. Felton his business card.

"If either of you think of anything later, or talk to anyone who might have seen Mr. Elliott arrive home Friday evening, please give us a call."

As the detectives stepped outside, Dr. Felton followed.

"I hate to say this, but I think you've got your man."

FOWLER AND JENKINS KNOCKED on the doors of the homes nearest to the crime scene. No one had seen Rand Elliott arrive home Friday night, and not a single neighbor knew the Elliotts well enough to comment on the couple's marriage, other than to say they seemed busy and successful.

Fowler asked Fred Owens, the owner of the garbage can where the knife was found, when he'd rolled the 50-gallon trash receptacle to the curb.

"I always put it out late in the afternoon, around five-thirty," the slightly-built, Wally Cox-looking man replied. "I don't like seeing those gigantic cans at the curb any longer than necessary."

"And what time is the garbage usually picked up?" Fowler asked.

"Between eight and nine on Saturday morning. They used to come before dawn, but the HOA board put an end to that last year."

It was the only information the detectives gathered other than the Feltons' criticism of Rand Elliott's chronic tardiness.

With the sun falling below the tree line, they decided to head back to the police station to update Chief Pierce and plot their next steps.

The detectives drove several minutes in silence, with Fowler's eyes fixed on the road ahead.

"What are you thinking so hard about?" Jenkins asked.

"We should call the Buncombe County Courthouse in Asheville to get a list of Sarah Elliott's cases," Fowler replied.

"You're still not convinced Elliott is guilty?"

"Even if he is, we should know what Sarah was doing the days and weeks before her death. Focusing on one suspect this early in the investigation isn't a good idea. You can bet the ponytailed defense attorney will be looking for other suspects, if for no other reason, to create reasonable doubt."

"I can make a call to the courthouse. I know the Clerk of Courts in Asheville," Jenkins said. "Her name's Betty Bronson. I played basketball with her older brother at North Carolina A&T many years ago."

"I didn't know you were an Aggie," Fowler said, turning to Jenkins with raised eyebrows.

"There are a lot of things you don't know about me," he said with a wry smile.

"Were you any good?"

"I wasn't exactly NBA material, but our team won the conference championship my senior year."

Fowler shook his head, grinning.

AFTER ARRIVING at the police station, Fowler went to Chief Pierce's office. Detective Jenkins continued down the hallway to his cubicle in the bullpen.

Pierce was at his desk leafing through a pile of folders when Fowler entered.

"You guys have had a long day," Pierce said. "Anything new?"

"Elliott claims to have an alibi," Fowler replied as he took a seat across from Pierce. "Claims he was at a bar in Charlotte waiting for a client who didn't show. According to him, he left around seven-thirty and arrived home shortly before nine."

"If he had a cellphone, his story should be easy to verify," Pierce said.

"There's the catch. Elliott shut off his phone after talking to his client at six-thirty. He says late Friday calls are always bad news."

"Not being able to verify his whereabouts will be *worse* news for him," Pierce replied. "What did you find out from his neighbors?"

"Not much. No one saw him come home Friday night, nor has anyone noticed unusual activity at the Elliotts' house," Fowler replied. "The only insight we got regarding their relationship was from Dr. Felton and his wife. The doctor claims Elliott was a lady's man who was suspiciously late to most events, but he didn't have much to back it up."

"Have you called Elliott's client or the place where they planned to meet?" Pierce asked.

"Not yet. Her name's Beth Adams and they were to meet at Fool's Gold, a small nightclub north of Charlotte."

"It sounds like Dr. Felton may have Elliott pegged," Pierce remarked.

A rap at the door was followed by Detective Jenkins entering the office. He paused, standing at the doorway.

"I talked to my friend at the courthouse," Jenkins began. "Not sure what all this means, but Sarah Elliott was defending a dealer named Malone Motts. He goes by Double M on the streets. Years ago, he was arrested on minor drug possession charges. This time he was pulled over in Asheville with five kilos of fentanyl in his trunk. He claims it was planted."

"Doesn't sound like a case Sarah Elliott would take," Fowler said. "I thought she was the defender of the poor and wrongly accused. This guy appears to be neither."

"It may be hard to find out much about this case," Jenkins continued. "Motts was found dead inside his cell at the county detention center this morning. It appears to be an overdose."

"How is a suspected drug dealer allowed access to drugs in jail?" Pierce asked. "Just on the surface, it's suspicious."

"With five hundred inmates and visitors coming and going. it's hard to screen for something as small as pills," Jenkins replied. "A dose of fentanyl the size of a couple grains of salt can kill you."

"Did your friend tell you any more about Motts?" Fowler asked.

"She was hesitant to say anything that wasn't public record. She did say he had a rap sheet, but that he'd kept his nose clean for several years."

"It's getting late," Pierce said "Go see what you can find out about Mr. Motts, and we'll get back together early tomorrow."

"Can you handle the computer searches?" Fowler asked Jenkins. "I think I'll try to catch Watkins at his law office and see what he might know about Sarah Elliott's clients."

- DAY 3 -

Sunday

DETECTIVE JENKINS ARRIVED at the police station ahead of Fowler for their Sunday morning meeting with Chief Pierce. A skeleton crew staffed the station as a half dozen officers patrolled the streets of Stonefield on the quiet weekend.

The senior detective sat in Pierce's conference room wearing creased slacks with his dress shirt peeking out beneath a dark blue cardigan. A steaming cup of coffee was set on the table before him as he read printouts from the criminal records database that he'd gathered the night before.

Jenkins was about to take his first sip of coffee when Fowler burst into the room dressed in faded jeans and a grey sweatshirt with U.S. Army printed in four-inch-high black letters across the front. A newspaper was folded under his arm.

Jenkins gingerly returned his hot cup back to the table.

"I just passed the chief in the parking lot," Fowler said. "He'll be here in a minute, and he won't be happy if he's seen this."

Fowler unfolded the Sunday edition of *The Daily Record* on the table. The headline read, *Client of Murdered Attorney Found Dead in Prison Cell.* A photo of Sarah Elliott was positioned beside the mug shot of a young black man.

"What does the article say?" Jenkins asked.

"They offer no evidence of a connection between Motts' death and the Elliott murder. It's all inuendo, with dots that don't connect. Still, it will bring attention we don't need."

Fowler focused on the printouts in front of Jenkins.

"Looks like your friend at the courthouse was right. Motts has an extensive rap sheet."

"From what I've found, he's not exactly a Boy Scout, but he's not the typical gangbanger either," Jenkins replied.

Pierce rushed in, wearing a snug-fitting dark suit and a scowl.

"Let's get rolling," he said. "Apparently, I have a niece being baptized this morning, and my wife wants me at the church in less than an hour."

"Before we start, have you read this?" Fowler asked, rotating the newspaper toward Pierce.

"Yeah. It's all bullshit intended to sell newspapers. It'll force me to have another press briefing, but let me worry about that."

Pierce folded the newspaper and pushed it aside.

"Now what have you found?" he asked, taking a seat.

"I was just telling Fowler that Motts isn't a typical drug-pushing gangbanger," Jenkins began.

"How so?" Pierce asked.

"For one, he graduated from App State ten years ago with a degree in business administration."

"How'd you learn that?" Fowler asked.

"I pulled testimony and pleadings from an earlier trial. There was a ton of personal information discussed."

"Did any of it explain how a college graduate ends up overdosing in a jail cell?" Pierce asked.

"His life took a turn when his parents were killed in a private plane crash during his senior year," Jenkins continued. "Motts grew up in Charlotte, living in an upscale neighborhood. But it turned out his family's lifestyle had been purchased with credit. After his parents' deaths, it became apparent his dad was deeply in debt. Instead of receiving an inheritance, Motts found himself struggling to pay for his final year of college."

"Where's he been since graduating?" Pierce asked.

"He drifted for several years--in and out of jobs and several run-ins with the law. Most recently he's been running MedEX Pharmaceuticals, a drug manufacturer in Charlotte that makes pain medications," Jenkins replied.

"Is the company on the up and up?" Fowler asked.

"MedEX is a privately held company, and it appears to be legit, but it's recently alleged to have connections with Cap INC, a conglomerate based in Charlotte owning and operating a variety of businesses."

"Where did you hear that?" Fowler asked. "I doubt from court testimony and pleadings."

"I found the connection to Cap INC in an obscure business article while searching for info on MedEX. The article said Cap INC has recently come under investigation by the DOJ and IRS for tax evasion and money laundering. Nothing has yet to be proven, but the company is suspected of laundering funds from illicit activities ranging from drug trafficking to prostitution."

"Sounds like a front for crime rings," Fowler said. "What's its connection to MedEX?"

"The article wasn't clear. It only stated the business relationship between Cap INC and several companies, including

MedEX, were a part of the recent federal investigation. More to come."

There was silence as everyone absorbed what Jenkins had uncovered.

"Sarah Elliott must've known about MedEX and its possible link to organized crime," Fowler said. "If so, why would she take the case? I thought she defended the poor and wrongly accused."

"On the surface, MedEX appears to be clean," Jenkins said. "I found no criminal or civil filings against the company, and I had to dig deep to find the report on the IRS investigation. It's likely Sarah didn't even know about Cap INC."

"Good point," Pierce added. "And none of this is evidence that her murder had anything to do with Malone Motts or MedEX."

"True," Fowler said. "But you have to admit, Sarah's association with Motts and his possible connections to organized crime complicates the case against her husband."

"I disagree," Pierce argued. "We have a murder weapon, fingerprints, and a motive of alleged infidelity. What more do we need?"

"The motive still lacks evidence," Jenkins said.

"I got with Eldon Watkins yesterday after our meeting," Fowler said. "He's an experienced criminal attorney. You can bet he's going to probe into Motts' potential links to organized crime, if for no other reason than to cloud the case against his client."

"So, what are you suggesting?" Pierce asked.

"We need to stay a step ahead of Watkins," Fowler replied. "I recommend we dig into what Malone Motts was doing prior to his arrest."

"Go ahead," said Pierce, "but don't lose sight of the case against Elliott. You still need to check out his alibi."

Fowler turned to Jenkins.

"I'm sure we can handle both. And besides, I know someone in Charlotte who can help investigate Motts and MedEX."

- 3.1 -

AS PIERCE HURRIED to his niece's baptism, Fowler and Jenkins headed down the hall to an empty detectives' bullpen.

Two rows of five cubicles faced each other, separated by a five-foot-high partition. The more senior investigators sat on the row with large floor-to-ceiling windows to their backs. The rookies' cubicles backed up to a long wall of file cabinets.

Even though Fowler was one of the more experienced and decorated detectives in the unit, his time on the force didn't rise to the level required for the senior row. It was a sore spot with him. He believed accomplishments should determine status in the bullpen, not tenure. It wasn't something he discussed with the other detectives, but Chief Pierce was well aware of Fowler's dissatisfaction.

The cubicles of the two detectives faced each other on the far end. Fowler took a seat and waited for Jenkins to pull his chair around to meet with him.

"I assume you're going to talk to Angela Jones about helping us with Motts," Jenkins said.

"Yeah, and the timing might be good. She was just assigned to head a task force with CMPD looking into street gang crime in Charlotte."

Jenkins paused.

"I met Detective Jones briefly about a year ago when she was working the Butcher Road cases with you. She's impressive."

"Very," Fowler replied.

"I was at my desk when she approached. I wasn't having a good day, and I think she sensed it. Anyway, she asked me how I was doing and how I liked working on the Stonefield Police Force. I told her that I'd had a good career, but I was approaching sixty and looking forward to retiring soon."

Fowler nervously tapped his foot on the floor, trying to hurry the story along. Unfazed, Jenkins continued.

"She told me I should reconsider retirement. That I provided an example for others to follow. She said that it was her grandfather being the first black SBI detective who convinced her to become a cop. Her comments were quite persuasive."

"She can definitely be persuasive," Fowler added.

"So, what's the story with you and her?" Jenkins asked. "Rumor has it you two were getting married last year. What happened?"

Fowler's glare was immediate.

"Okay. Let's get back to work," he said. "Why don't you see if you can get a hold of the client Elliott claims he was to meet on Friday night, and I'll head back down the hall to call Detective Jones."

Returning to the conference room, Fowler placed the call.

Seventy miles away, Angela Jones set her book on a side table and rose from a thick cushioned chair. She hadn't changed from her pajama pants and sweatshirt since waking an hour ago.

"Hey, Jack," she answered. "What's up?"

"Does something have to be *up* for me to give you a call?" Fowler teased. "Can't I just call to see how my favorite SBI detective is doing?"

"You could, but I doubt you did."

"You're right. I need your help getting the dirt on a former Charlotte gang member. His name's Malone Motts."

"Double-M?" she asked, surprised.

"You know him?"

"I know *of* him," she replied. "His rep on the street is he's smart, tough, and working his way up."

"Working his way up? What do you mean?" Fowler asked.

"Street gangs aren't what they used to be, Jack. It isn't always the biggest and baddest who rule. There's a hierarchy, and you gain power through influence and your ability to generate business, albeit illegal business."

"And this Motts generated business for the gangs?"

"That's what I understand. He and others like him are recruited in an effort to legitimize gang-related activities."

"This sounds more like organized crime than street gangs," Fowler said.

"Well, the model is similar. They disguise illegal activity with what appear to be valid businesses, and some actually are legitimate. Maybe not moral, but legal."

"Do you know what Motts has been up to recently?"

"Last I heard, he was working for MedEX, a pharmaceutical company," she replied. "Why all the interest in Motts?"

"The attorney in the murder case I'm working was defending him when she was killed, and now Motts is dead. He overdosed in his cell."

"Really? From what I know of this guy, overdosing doesn't sound like something he'd do," Jones said. "He was making drugs, not taking them."

"Can you get more detail on Motts and what he was up to before landing in the Buncombe County Jail?"

"I'll ask around, but my usual informants are better with getting info on street gangs, not so much with organized crime," she replied. "I thought the husband was charged with the murder. Are you now thinking Motts and his company may have played a role?"

"Not sure," he replied. "There are definitely unanswered questions about Rand Elliott and his motive for killing his wife. Jenkins is checking into Elliott's alibi. He claims he was to meet with a client in Charlotte at a nightclub and was driving home when his wife was murdered."

"Sounds like your investigation is headed my direction," Jones said.

"There's a good chance Jenkins and I will need to take a road trip to Charlotte soon."

"Overnight by any chance?" she asked.

Fowler chuckled.

"And what would we do with Jenkins?"

"You're right. Bad idea," she replied.

"You had your chance to get assigned to this case and you opted to head that joint task force," Fowler said. "Any chance you could get reassigned given the potential link to Motts and MedEX?"

"First of all, I was *assigned* to the task force. I didn't *opt* to head it," she said. "Second, my boss isn't going to reassign me unless..."

"Unless what?" he asked.

"Unless we can prove Motts and MedEX are clearly involved in the Elliott murder."

"So, you're in?"

"Yeah. I'll at least find out what Motts was up to," she replied. "My boss, Lieutenant Alvarez, will determine my role going forward."

"Sounds good. Let me know if you need any help convincing Alvarez."

"First things first," she said. "I'll get back to you as soon as I find out anything on Motts."

"Great."

"So, am I still your favorite SBI detective?" she asked.

"Second place isn't even close. See you soon."

Fowler stepped back to the detectives' bullpen where he saw Jenkins place his phone back onto his desk.

"How'd it go?" Fowler asked.

"It appears Beth Adams screens her calls," Jenkins replied. "I left a voicemail introducing myself and stating I needed to talk with her regarding Rand Elliott. She called back a couple minutes later."

"Well, at least she's cooperating."

"Not really," Jenkins replied. "Before I could ask my first question, she said she was uncomfortable talking with me over the phone. And if we really needed to speak with her, she would arrange a meeting with her attorney present."

"Lawyering up to answer questions about a cancelled business meeting? That's suspicious," Fowler said. "I'm beginning to wonder about Rand Elliott's relationship with Ms. Adams."

"I hope your discussion with Detective Jones had better results."

"She'd heard of Motts and agreed to dig into what he was up to prior to his arrest," Fowler replied.

"Is the SBI onboard with her working the case?" Jenkins asked.

"Not yet, but I'm hoping her lieutenant will agree if we can link Motts or MedEX to the murder."

"That's a big if," Jenkins said.

Fowler thought, staring past his partner.

"Not much we can do on a Sunday, but let's plan on meeting tomorrow with Beth Adams and her attorney," he said.

"What about Detective Jones?" Jenkins asked.

"We need to give her time to work with her informants, but I'll give her a call while we're in Charlotte."

- DAY 4 -

Monday

BETH ADAMS WASN'T available until mid-afternoon. She arranged a meeting at her attorney's office in south Charlotte, five miles from her office at Delco Pharmaceuticals. Fowler and Jenkins arrived at the law offices of Blake & Edwards precisely at 3:15. The parking lot was filled with sleek, late-model autos, mostly foreign. Fowler's giant sedan stuck out like a fat man at a salad buffet.

In stark contrast to Eldon Watkins' second floor office on Main Street in Stonefield, the offices of Blake & Edwards reeked of opulence. The glass doors leading into the three-story mirrored building slid to the side as Fowler and Jenkins stepped into the marble-floored lobby. They were greeted by a receptionist wearing a snug black suit with a low-cut blouse and bold silver necklace that caused Fowler to nervously divert his eyes elsewhere.

"How may I help you?" she asked, scanning the detectives from head to toe.

"We're here to meet with Beth Adams and her attorney, Benjamin Blake," Fowler replied.

"Mr. Blake is expecting you. He's on the third floor in suite 301. You can't miss it. Take the elevators over there."

Blake's office looked like the entrance to the Delta frequent flyer lounge at Atlanta's Hartsfield-Jackson Airport. Behind a wall of glass sat another stunning receptionist at a granite top desk. She was framed by a dark teak wall to her rear displaying clocks from around the world.

"Good afternoon, gentlemen," she greeted. "Ms. Adams and Mr. Blake are waiting in his conference room. First door to the left down this corridor."

The door was ajar, so Fowler knocked lightly and stepped inside.

Ben Blake immediately rose from his chair at the far end of the conference table. Beth Adams remained seated to his left in a high back leather chair.

Wearing a black, pin-striped Armani suit, the fit attorney with thick silver hair extended his hand, first to Fowler and then to Jenkins.

"Good afternoon, detectives. I'm Ben Blake and this is Beth Adams. Our firm represents Delco Pharmaceuticals, so she asked that I join her today."

The detectives nodded toward the woman dressed in a dark blue business suit and white blouse. With short blonde hair, porcelain complexion and blue eyes, Adams strikingly resembled Sarah Elliott.

"I'm Detective Jack Fowler and this is my partner Detective Brooks Jenkins. We're with Stonefield PD."

"Please have a seat. Can I get you a cup of coffee or anything else before we begin?" Blake asked as he extended his arm toward the chairs across from Ms. Adams.

"No thanks," Fowler replied. Jenkins shook his head.

They all settled into their seats.

"Why don't you start by telling us specifically why you're here," Blake suggested.

"Before we begin, do you mind if Detective Jenkins takes a few notes?"

"That's fine," Blake replied. "And I should tell you everything in this room is recorded."

Fowler glanced up. Small cameras in the upper corners of the room were discretely blended into the molding.

"Like my partner told Ms. Adams on the phone, Rand Elliott has been charged with the murder of his wife, Sarah," Fowler began. "He denies killing his wife and claims he was to meet with Ms. Adams that evening at Fool's Gold, a nightclub in north Charlotte. We're here to better understand Ms. Adams' relationship with Mr. Elliott and to get her account of what Mr. Elliott has told us."

"You understand that my client and Mr. Elliott never met the evening in question," Blake said.

"Yes, but we do have questions about a phone call or calls Ms. Adams may have exchanged that evening with Mr. Elliott, the subject of the calls, and the purpose of their proposed meeting at Fool's Gold," Fowler replied. "May I continue?"

Blake nodded.

"Are you married, Ms. Adams?"

"Yes, our tenth anniversary is next week. Are you married, Detective?"

"No, but that's not relevant to our discussion," Fowler replied.

"Neither is my marital status."

Fowler paused and took in a deep breath.

"Did you have plans to meet with Mr. Elliott at Fool's Gold this past Friday evening? And if so, why and at what time?"

"I had a meeting in Asheville the coming weekend. Several other officers from Delco and I were to hold a strategic planning session at the Grove Park Inn beginning Saturday morning. We conduct these meetings every year," she calmly began.

"And how does all this relate to your proposed meeting with Mr. Elliott?"

"Rand Elliott is the marketing director for a company that sells diagnostic equipment used in our development of new pharmaceuticals. He'd asked to meet with me earlier on Friday to discuss a delay in delivery of equipment we were expecting. My calendar was booked, but being a persistent salesman, he asked if I could meet him after work. I told him I was headed to Asheville, and after a brief discussion, I picked a familiar location for us to meet."

"How long was the meeting to last?"

"Rand asked for an hour," she replied. "I was to arrive around six-thirty."

"A nightclub strikes me as an unconventional place to discuss business," Fowler said. "Why there?"

"Like I said, it was on my way to Asheville, and I happened to know it had a relatively quiet bar with booths where we could discuss business."

"So, you'd been there before?" Fowler asked.

"Yes."

"To conduct business?"

Adams turned to her attorney, looking for help.

"I don't see why you need to know the purpose of my client's prior meetings at this establishment," Blake argued.

"Have you ever met Mr. Elliott there before?" Fowler asked.

"No," she snapped.

"Have you ever met Mr. Elliott at other locations after work?"

She paused.

"I'm a busy executive. My schedule often requires I extend my normal workday and conduct meetings after hours."

"And that includes with Mr. Elliott?"

She nodded.

"Did Mr. Elliott cancel your meeting Friday night or did you?"

"I called him around six-thirty to cancel," she replied.

"May I ask the reason?"

"I was running late and couldn't get packed in time for my weekend trip."

"Have you spoken with him since?"

"No."

Fowler paused, looking down at notes he'd placed on the table.

"Mr. Elliott claims he frequently turns off his cellphone after leaving work on Fridays. Can you verify this?"

A glare sprang to her face.

"What?" she asked.

"Have you ever tried to reach him on a Friday evening and found his phone powered off?"

"I don't make a habit of calling salesmen on Friday evenings if that's what you're asking."

"Has Mr. Elliott ever made you uncomfortable by flirting with you or with other women in your presence?" Fowler asked.

"No, and I hope that ridiculous question indicates you're finished."

"Unless you have something that clearly relates to your investigation, I suggest we stop here," Blake said, pushing back from the table.

Fowler looked to Jenkins. His senior partner glanced at his notes and nodded.

"That's all," Fowler replied, standing. "Thank you both for your time."

THE DETECTIVES QUIETLY exited the building.

"You think she's telling the truth?" Fowler asked as they reached the parking lot.

"Probably, but I think there's more she's *not* telling us."

"Agreed," Fowler said. "And I get the impression her relationship with Elliott extends beyond his sales calls. She slipped up at least once and called him Rand."

"And when you asked if Elliott ever flirted with her, the question hit a nerve. She quickly bristled," Jenkins added.

"Still, all we have is circumstantial evidence and hearsay. We have nothing that proves Elliott was cheating on his wife, and his alibi is still intact."

Fowler's phone chirped and he pulled it from his coat pocket. It was Detective Jones.

"I think I may have a lead on Motts," she said.

"What have you learned?"

"Nothing yet. Blade Jackson, one of my informants, has agreed to meet with me along with an associate of Motts."

"Who's the associate?"

"Blade wouldn't give me a name."

"How did you get that arranged so quickly?"

"I promised Blade that I could get his cousin out of county jail on a reduced bail. I know the DA. Given the situation, I think he'll agree."

"What if he doesn't?"

"Then I can forget about using Blade in the future."

"When's the meeting?"

"Tonight at seven. He prefers to meet at this warehouse on the north edge of Charlotte where he can make sure I'm alone. We've met there before."

"I'm still in town. Is there any way I could go with you?"

"I wouldn't advise it. You might spook him and blow the whole meeting. I'll have backup a few minutes away if anything happens."

Fowler paused.

"Jenkins and I are planning to stop by the nightclub that Elliott's using as his alibi. How about I ask Jenkins to drop me off at a rental car agency and then meet you at your place later. I'd like to hear what happens."

"And make sure I'm safe?" she asked.

"Yeah. That, too."

"I won't get back home until nine, or maybe even later."

"I know the passcode. Not a problem," Fowler said.

"Okay. I better get on my way," she said. "See you then."

Fowler stuffed the phone back into his pocket.

"Angela has a lead on Motts," he said. "She's meeting one of her informants at seven. I'd like to be at her place when she returns to see what she finds out. There's a car rental place near the nightclub. Just drop me off there after we're done, and I'll rent a car. You can drive the Grey Ghost back home."

"I don't want to drive this beast back to Stonefield," Jenkins replied. "Keep your car, and I'll take Uber back. But if there are any issues regarding the expenses back at SPD, you're paying."

- 4.1 -

FOOL'S GOLD WAS EXACTLY what Fowler expected. Popular in the 1990s, the glitz and glamor of the nightclub had long since waned. The marquee out front looked like a partially solved *Wheel of Fortune* puzzle with several letters missing.

The club wasn't open on Mondays, but Fowler had arranged a meeting with the manager. It was approaching 5:30 and delivery vehicles were bringing food and beverages to side doors in preparation for the week ahead. A cleaning crew washed down the front of the stucco building with high-pressure hoses. Fowler and Jenkins dodged the spray as they maneuvered toward the front door.

The wide glass doors at the entrance were unlocked. Fowler pushed them aside. The detectives stepped inside to find the building vacant, not a person in sight. The only illumination was from fire escape lighting.

The main room was straight ahead, down a wide corridor. The shadowy nightclub was dead quiet and looked like a movie set from a horror film.

Chairs were turned upside down on top of a dozen round tables. The stage loomed several feet above an open dance floor that extended the width of the room. Electrical cords, ropes, and unlit spotlights hung from a catwalk over the stage.

"Anyone here?" Fowler called out, his voice echoing back.

"One minute," someone replied from a distance.

Footsteps grew louder as a female figure approached from across the ballroom floor. A conservatively dressed, auburn haired woman in her 30s stepped out of the darkness and flipped a light switch, illuminating the corridor.

"You must be the detectives from Stonefield," she said. "I'm Tina, the club's floor manager. Mr. Reynolds was called away and asked that I meet with you."

"I'm Detective Fowler."

"And I'm Detective Jenkins."

"Mr. Reynolds said you had questions about one of our patrons who was here Friday night," she began.

"That's right. His name is Rand Elliott. We were hoping to talk to someone who might be able to confirm he was here that night," Fowler said as he extended a recent mug shot.

"I was working the floor then," she said. "Let me take a close look."

She moved directly beneath an overhead light and held up the photo.

"I didn't see him here Friday night," she said. "But I've seen him here before, several times, in fact."

"Are you sure?"

"I'm pretty sure. If it's the same fella, he's a little over six feet tall, light hair, good build, and a talkative guy."

"Ever remember seeing him with anyone?" Fowler asked.

"He rarely comes alone, and if he does, he isn't alone very long," she replied with a sly grin. "I've thought about approaching him before, but Mr. Reynolds frowns on employees socializing with the customers."

"Is there anyone else around who might be able to tell us if Elliott was here Friday? It would've been from around six-thirty to seven-thirty."

"Paul Zeller was in the bar earlier stocking shelves," she replied. "I think he was tending bar that night."

"Can you point us in his direction?" Fowler asked.

"Follow me."

The shapely floor manager headed down the corridor and turned to the right before reaching the main room. They entered a dark, spacious area decorated like a Western saloon. At the far side, overhead lights illuminated a long, wooden bar. An open door behind the bar led to a storage area.

"Paul, you still here?" Tina called out.

A muscular man wearing jeans and a snug dark t-shirt came through the door. His head was shaved and tattoos covered his beefy forearms.

"What's up, Tina?"

"Detectives Fowler and Jenkins are here to meet with Mr. Reynolds, but he was called away. Do you have a minute? They have questions about one of our customers."

"I'll do whatever I can," the stocky man replied, wiping his hands with a bar towel. "Don't want to upset the cops."

"Did you happen to notice this man here on Friday night around six-thirty?"

The bartender took the photo from Fowler and held it under the lights above the bar.

"Yeah. He was here. He seemed to be in a hurry. I remember he had a drink, took a phone call, and then left. He sat right there," Paul said, pointing to a chair at the end of the bar.

"Any idea of the time that he left?" Fowler asked.

"It was before seven, because I only worked a partial shift that night, and I was on my way home around then."

"You're sure of this?" Jenkins asked.

"Positive. Why?"

"Your testimony may be required if this man goes to trial," Jenkins replied. "He claims he didn't leave the bar until after seven-thirty, making it difficult for him to have committed the crime he's accused of."

"And what crime is that?" the bartender asked.

"He's accused of killing his wife."

"Shit! That guy I served is a murderer?"

"And he's married?" Tina scowled. "Am I ever glad I stayed clear of him."

"He's only been accused at this point," Fowler clarified.

"Do you think I'll really need to testify?" the bartender asked.

"It's possible. If so, you'll be subpoenaed well in advance."

Fowler glanced at his watch.

"You've been very helpful, but we need to go," he said, turning to leave.

"Can you find your way out?" Tina asked.

"Sure. Thanks again."

The detectives stepped quickly outside to the parking lot. The sun had set during the time they were inside. Overhead street lights cast their shadows onto the dark asphalt as they walked toward Fowler's cruiser. They paused before entering the car.

"If Elliott left here before seven, that shoots a huge hole in his alibi," Jenkins said.

"It definitely puts him arriving home within the window established as his wife's time of death."

"Sounds like Beth Adams was lying about her relationship with Elliott," Jenkins said. "Should we double back and confront her?"

"Maybe later," Fowler replied. "She's probably just hiding all this from her husband and her employer. It's not clear she had anything to do with Sarah Elliott's murder."

"You're probably right."

"I'm gonna head on over to Jones' place. Are you sure you want to take Uber back to Stonefield?" Fowler asked.

"Yeah. I'll call them from here. You go ahead."

- 4.2 -

RUNWAY LIGHTS OUTLINING the driveway greeted Fowler as he approached Jones' modern single-story home. It had been several weeks since he'd visited her northeast Charlotte residence, tucked in a middle-class neighborhood.

After keying in Detective Jones' badge number, the garage door lifted slowly. Once inside, Fowler lowered the door and flipped on the back hall lights. Six-thirty was brightly displayed on the microwave clock as he entered the kitchen. He figured Jones would be well on her way to the warehouse by then.

He grabbed a soda from the refrigerator and sat at the kitchen table. After a few swigs, he pulled out his cellphone and tapped *Angela* at the top of his address book.

He and Jones had set their cellphones to allow location tracking. The map on his phone indicated she'd just departed the SBI district office and was less than 20 minutes south of the meeting location she'd given him.

The thought of Angela driving alone at night to a remote warehouse didn't sit well, but he knew she'd be furious if he intervened. Her persistent drive to prove she could excel in a field dominated by men constantly collided with his protective instincts.

It's just a meeting to gather information. It's not like she's going on a drug bust.

The thought did little to calm him. He wondered if he'd be able to wait two hours to hear the outcome of the meeting.

DETECTIVE JONES DROVE her late-model, blue Volvo north on U.S. Route 29 with her backup a safe distance to the rear. She wore a transmitter inside her jacket that communicated with the two agents following her.

She'd been instructed to be unarmed and alone when she arrived. Her plan was to remove the jacket and set it aside before she was searched, showing that she was unarmed and hopefully diverting attention from the transmitter.

Minutes later, she turned off the highway and onto a county road. She passed fewer and fewer cars the further she drove into the darkness.

Pop! Pop! Pop!

A flourish of gunshots pierced the silence of the countryside. The rapid explosions sounded like automatic weapon fire coming from a short distance ahead.

Seconds later, she came upon a lone car near an intersection, tipping nose first into the ditch beside the road. Jones coasted closer before stopping and reaching into the glovebox for her .38 caliber Smith & Wesson. She stepped from the car and approached with her gun extended.

The windshield and a side window of the vehicle had been shattered and several bullet holes pierced the body of the car. The bloodied face of Blade Jackson, her informant, was pressed against the steering wheel. His eyes were fixed open, staring toward her. A bullet hole dripped blood from his forehead. A second man was slumped in the seat on the passenger side, his body riddled with gunshot wounds.

"Hurry ahead! I'm at a crossroads," she shouted into the transmitter. "Blade Jackson never made it to the warehouse. He and his friend are dead--ambushed at this intersection."

THE SHOOTERS could have fled from the intersection in any of three different directions—north, east or west. It wasn't immediately obvious to Detective Jones or the agents in the backup unit which way they went, although given the terrain and the fact Jones didn't see headlights leave the scene, the killers probably fled north over a slight rise. In any case, it was too late to give chase.

It took less than ten minutes for NC State Police and an ambulance to arrive. Fifteen minutes later, the forensic team and coroner were on-site to process the bodies and collect whatever evidence could be gathered.

Strobing police lights, roadside flares, and generator-powered floodlights lit up the deadly intersection. The few vehicles that approached were quickly sent in the opposite direction without explanation. What had been a remote country crossroads had become a bustling crime scene.

Back at Jones' home, Fowler could see her cellphone signal frozen at the intersection for an extended period. Fearing something had gone terribly wrong, he called.

Jones' phone rang five time before she was able to pick up.

"I'm okay," she answered. "But Blade Jackson wasn't so lucky. He and his friend were ambushed and killed."

"Damn! What can I do?" Fowler asked, his heart racing.

"I can't think of anything. It'll take a while to process the carnage out here and fill out my report, but I should be home in a couple hours. If you prefer to head back to Stonefield, I'd understand."

"No. I'll be here," he replied. "Any ID on the guy with Jackson? I'm just wondering about his connection to Motts. If you have a name, it would give me something to research while I'm waiting."

"No identification was found on the body, and no one recognizes him. But it shouldn't take long in the morning to match his fingerprints or do a facial scan against the felony database. The guy's face wasn't mangled too badly."

"Sounds like I'll just have to wait here."

"I'll be there as soon as I can. See you later," she said, turning her attention back to the crime scene.

After an hour of searching the area, little evidence was uncovered. Multiple AR-15 bullet casings were sprayed across the road and each was marked with a yellow tent card. Based on the large number of bullet holes in the car and the victims, most of the casings must have ejected inside the shooters' car.

It appeared the killers never stepped outside their vehicle. No footprints were left behind. From the pattern of bullet holes, it appeared the intersection was blocked by the assailants' car. Gunfire was directed at the front and left side of the victims' vehicle, forcing the car to careen to the right and into the ditch.

THE RISING GARAGE DOOR awakened Jack from the living room sofa. Glancing at his watch, it took a second for his eyes to determine it was just past 11:30. He quickly rose to greet Angela coming down the back hallway.

Even after a 16-hour workday that included processing a gruesome murder scene on a chilly autumn night, a smile formed on Angela's face as she approached.

Fowler gathered her into his arms and they held each other.

"What the hell happened tonight?" he asked, stepping back from their embrace.

"I'm not sure, but it seems someone didn't want Blade Jackson and his friend to meet with me."

"Did Jackson give any indication the meeting would put him in danger?"

"No. Our discussion was short," she replied. "All I told him was I wanted to speak with someone who knew what Malone Motts was doing prior to his recent arrest."

"And that was it?"

"Pretty much. Jackson called back the next day saying he found someone, and all he wanted in return was to lower the bond on his cousin."

"What about the guy who knew Motts? What was he getting out of this?"

"He never said, and now that he's dead, we may never know," she replied.

"After my meeting at the nightclub this afternoon, I was becoming convinced Rand Elliott killed his wife, but a lot of people associated with Malone Motts are getting killed."

"Do you think Rand Elliott is tied up with Motts in some way?" Angela asked.

"I see absolutely no connection, other than Elliott's wife was representing Motts."

"Maybe this is all coincidental, and the murder of Elliott's wife has nothing to do with Malone Motts."

"My head is spinning. I suggest we go to bed and get a fresh start in the morning."

"Sounds like a great idea," she replied. "But I need a quick shower to clean off all this road grime."

"I'll wait for you."

- DAY 5 -

Tuesday

ANGELA WAS STILL HALF ASLEEP when she reached across the bed to feel a warm depression in the mattress.

He couldn't have gone far, she thought.

With her eyes half open, she turned to look at the blinds over the window. The sun had yet to rise. She clumsily reached for the clock on the nightstand and turned it toward her. She lay wondering when Jack would return.

Minutes later, the smell of bacon and eggs drifted down the hall and into the bedroom, followed by the clatter of dishes.

What's he up to?

Angela pushed herself up and swung her legs to the side of the bed. She sat there for a moment, considering falling back onto the warm mattress. Wearing Jack's t-shirt, which hit her mid-thigh, she rose from the bed and shuffled down the hall toward the kitchen.

She found Jack, spatula in hand and fully dressed in his previous day's attire. He was busy assembling breakfast and didn't hear her coming until she spoke.

"What are you doing?" she asked, her short black hair askew and arms hanging limply at her side. "Has it gotten to the point where you prefer food over staying in bed with me a few extra minutes?"

"That will never happen," he replied. "But I have an early meeting with Pierce and the DA, and I can't face them on an empty stomach."

She stared at Jack for a few seconds, allowing her head to clear.

"I guess you're right. I should go into the office and make sure they're able to ID the other dead guy," she said, stepping to the kitchen table. "But for future reference, I need at least six hours of sleep, and neither of us came close to that last night."

"Point taken," he replied.

Jack placed a plate of eggs and toast with a glass of juice in front of Angela and took a seat across from her.

"I'm sure I'll be assigned to follow up on the double murder last night," Angela said. "Have you thought about what your next steps will be on the Elliott case?"

"It seems Elliott wasn't telling the truth about the time he left the nightclub. The bartender will testify to him leaving before seven, allowing plenty of time for Elliott to get home and kill his wife before eight."

"You sound like you're still not sure he did it."

"It's possible he's guilty, but I've never been convinced," he replied.

"Why?"

"What's his motive? He's a womanizer, but that doesn't make him a killer. And how sloppy can he be to leave the murder weapon with his prints where it was easily found?"

"You never answered my first question, Jack. What are your next steps?"

"After meeting with Pierce and the DA this morning, I think I'll pay a call on Elliott's attorney. I need to let him know the

77

case against his client firmed up yesterday. And unless Watkins can find another alibi or help us identify another killer, Elliott's going to prison."

- 5.1 -

FOWLER ARRIVED at the Stonefield Police Station a couple of minutes late. Chief Pierce and Ron Olsen, the recently elected DA, were just taking their seats when Fowler hurried into the conference room.

"Good morning," Fowler said.

Dressed in a business suit and white shirt, Olsen glanced down at his watch before giving Fowler a judgmental stare.

"I got a call from Detective Jenkins on my way in. He's under the weather this morning," Fowler said. "He thinks it might be the flu."

"I have a meeting at the courthouse in thirty minutes," the hawk-faced, balding DA interrupted. "This update needs to be quick."

Since being elected DA, Olsen had been a pain in Fowler's side. Fowler and Olsen were in the same Stonefield High graduating class, but from vastly different backgrounds. Fowler was the son of a police officer, Olsen the son of a multi-term state congressman. Fowler received his criminal justice degree from Piedmont Community College and then graduated from a 20-week police academy after serving in the U.S. Army. Olsen leveraged his father's political career to attend Duke Law School, graduating in the middle of his class.

"I'll be as brief as possible," Fowler said.

"I got your voicemail from late last night," Pierce replied. "It sounds like you've extended the Elliott murder investigation beyond the suspect in custody."

"I'll get to that, but the primary reason for going to Charlotte yesterday was to investigate Elliott's alibi," Fowler began. "Our interview with Beth Adams, the woman Elliott was supposed to meet the night of the murder, was somewhat uneventful. She admitted they had an appointment, but said she called Elliott and cancelled around 6:30."

"That was it?" Olsen asked. "You learned nothing else?"

"I got the feeling she and Elliott were more than just business associates."

"Go on," Pierce prodded.

"Our visit to the nightclub was more revealing. We found a bartender who's willing to testify Elliott arrived at the club around six-thirty and departed well before seven."

"So, if Elliott drove straight home, he could have arrived before eight," Pierce said.

"What about a motive?" Olsen asked. "Any new revelations?"

"It seems Elliott is a bit of a womanizer," Fowler replied. "He'd been seen at this nightclub on many occasions with different women."

"I guess that's better than nothing," Olsen said. "But it's not exactly a reason to kill his wife."

"We've got a murder weapon and fingerprints," Pierce argued, "and Detective Fowler just shot a wide hole in Elliott's alibi. What more do you need?"

Olsen ignored Pierce's comeback, instead turning to Fowler.

"What's this about you extending the murder investigation to other suspects?" Olsen asked.

"I found it more than a little strange that Sarah Elliott was murdered just hours before Malone Motts committed suicide in his jail cell."

"How does any of that relate to Rand Elliott?" Olsen asked.

"I'm not sure it does, but Motts had a criminal history in Charlotte, so I thought I'd ask Detective Jones to check into his recent activities."

"Why in the hell would you do that?" Olsen exploded. "Are you intentionally trying to create reasonable doubt in my case against Elliott?"

"I'm just trying to rule out other possible suspects," Fowler argued. "Elliott's attorney is sure to bring up the death of Sarah Elliott's client at trial."

"Has Detective Jones uncovered anything on Motts?" Pierce asked.

"One of Jones' informants found someone who knew Motts and was willing to meet with her at a secure location," Fowler said.

"What did she find out?" Olsen asked.

"Jones' informant and the man connected to Motts were both murdered on the way to meeting with her. It was a professional hit."

"And your wild theory is that Sarah Elliott and the two dead informants were killed by someone associated with Motts?" Olsen mocked.

"I haven't established a theory, Ron," Fowler replied. "But you have to admit these killings warrant further investigation."

"I don't have to admit *anything*. I have a murder suspect in custody and plenty of evidence to go to trial and convict him. It sounds like you're trying to find a reason to link my murder case to Charlotte crimes where neither you nor Chief Pierce have jurisdiction."

Ron Olsen turned to Chief Pierce, his face red with anger.

"If your detective screws up my case against Rand Elliott, I'll hold you personally responsible and make sure the mayor and city council understand what occurred."

"Don't threaten me," Pierce said, pushing his chair back and standing. "We both have jobs to do, and I suggest you let us do ours."

"I'll expect daily updates," Olsen said. "Have your detective notify my assistant if anything changes."

Olsen stomped from the conference room with his briefcase in hand.

"He's always been a pugnacious little prick," Fowler hissed.

Pierce settled back into his chair, his face still red from the near altercation.

"He does have a point," Pierce said, taking a handkerchief from his pocket and wiping the moisture from his neck. "The investigation of Malone Motts and the murder of Jones' informants *are* outside our jurisdiction."

"Not if Motts and these murders are connected to someone responsible for Sarah Elliott's murder," Fowler argued. "Then these cases would be linked."

"Even with everything you've uncovered, you're still not convinced Rand Elliott's guilty, are you?"

"He may very well be, but there are still too many unanswered questions."

Pierce paused.

"Okay, continue to work the Motts connection, but no trips outside of our jurisdiction without informing me in advance."

- 5.2 -

FOWLER KNEW IF RON OLSEN discovered he was sharing information with Elliott's defense attorney, the irritable DA would have a stroke. But Fowler figured there was nothing he was going to discuss with Eldon Watkins that the attorney wouldn't learn during pre-trial discovery.

Entering the lobby of Watkins' law office, he found the receptionist's desk unattended and dog-eared magazines scattered across a dusty coffee table in front of a well-worn sofa. Fowler heard a conversation behind Watkins' office door, so he stood and waited.

Several minutes passed before a little old lady with silver-blue hair and a quilted purse stepped from Watkins' office. She shuffled past Fowler, offering a brief smile, and then continued out the door and down the stairs.

Fowler entered Watkins' office.

"Another high-profile murder case?" he jested, not cracking a smile.

Seated at his desk wearing a corduroy jacket and open collar shirt, Watkins calmly looked up.

"Very funny. What brings you here?"

"I have information you might find useful."

"Have a seat," he said. "I have some time before going to meet with Elliott at your lovely jail."

"You might want to ask him about what I'm about to tell you," Fowler began. "I'll also be talking to Elliott about this later."

"Enough with the tease. What do you have to tell me this morning?"

"I spoke with Beth Adams, the client Elliott was supposed to meet with the night of the murder, and I also went to Fool's Gold and spoke with a floor manager and bartender who recognized Elliott's photo."

"Go on. What did they tell you?"

"That your client likes the ladies and that he lied about the time he left the nightclub. He departed before seven and could have easily arrived home and killed his wife within the timeframe established by the coroner."

"And you have proof of this?"

"I have a bartender who's certain he served Elliott one drink and that he left before seven."

Watkins paused.

"I'm checking surveillance cameras in the area of Elliott's home," Watkins replied. "I'm sure something will turn up to prove when Elliott arrived that night."

"We've already checked and found nothing," Fowler said.

He paused to let his news sink in.

"It appears the noose is tightening around the neck of your client."

"If you came up here just to gloat about the progress of your investigation, you've made your points and can leave now."

"I actually had another reason for coming to see you. I need information about Motts," Fowler said.

"Sarah was handling that case. We discussed the charges, but that was it."

"Surely there's a file that she kept on him," Fowler argued. "Can't you find it and fill me in?"

"If there's a file, it's either in Sarah's briefcase or locked in her office file cabinet. I have access to neither," Watkins replied. "And even if I did, all the information remains protected under the attorney-client privilege."

"The client and attorney are both dead," Fowler said defiantly. "Who needs protection?"

"There may be others related to the defendant who require this protection. Death of the client doesn't release the privilege, Detective."

"Then what the hell would release it?" Fowler asked, taking a step closer to Watkins.

"A court order is required. Not easily done. You'll need to show just cause to subpoena the information."

"Who has the key to Sarah's file cabinet?"

"I assume Sarah had the only key," Watkins replied. "I don't have a duplicate."

"Given your client is running out of options, I'd think you'd want to help find other suspects in Sarah Elliott's murder."

"And you believe Sarah's defense of Motts played a role in her death?"

"It's a long shot, but two more people were killed on their way to meet with Detective Jones in Charlotte. They were to provide information to Jones about Malone Motts."

"Interesting, but not much I can do about any of that," Watkins said. "If you want to learn more about the Motts case, I suggest you find Sarah's briefcase and the key to her file cabinet."

FOWLER RETURNED to the police station and placed a call to SBI Forensics in Greensboro. He asked for Inspector Jim Jennings, one of the two men who processed the Elliotts' home the night of the murder.

"Hi, Jim. This is Jack Fowler. I'm looking for something that doesn't show up on the evidence list gathered at the Elliott home."

"I'll help if I can, but we've listed anything that could be considered evidence."

"I'm specifically looking for three items: Sarah Elliott's briefcase, a file folder for a case she was working, and a key to her office file cabinet."

"I don't recall finding any of those," he replied.

"Are you sure?"

"They're something we would've tagged and noted," he replied. "I guess it's possible they were hidden or tucked away where we didn't see them. Maybe we just missed them."

Fowler's eyes popped open as he thought of something.

"Shit! Elliott took her SUV that night!" he cursed under his breath.

"What was that, Detective?"

"What about the Range Rover recovered after Elliott was arrested? Were any of these items found inside?" Fowler asked.

"No. The vehicle was clean. We searched it before Elliott took it that night."

"I guess that's all," Fowler said. "Thanks for your help."

He decided to check in with Detective Jones. After the second ring, she picked up her cellphone.

"Are the fingerprint results back yet?" he asked.

"You must be psychic," she replied. "I just received a report in my email a couple minutes ago."

"Was he anyone you knew?"

"No. The dead guy with my informant was Antonio Perez, Junior, a multiple offender, mainly drug offenses. He's not someone you'd think would associate with Malone Motts. They operated on two entirely different levels."

"Well, he must've known something about Motts that got him killed," Fowler replied.

"Seems so."

"Are there any associates of Perez you might contact to find out what he knew?"

"That's an obvious next step, but no names rise to the surface," she replied.

"Is there a Perez, Senior? Maybe his family is a place to start."

"I don't know, but I'll find out. Speaking of family, I discovered Malone Motts has a grandmother living in Charlotte. I thought I'd pay her a visit."

"You're kidding. Where's she live?"

"She's not in a nursing home like you might expect. She lives in a swanky townhome in NoDa."

"How are you balancing the gang task force with investigating the Motts case?"

"Good news on that front. Alvarez has reassigned the task force to another detective. After the double homicide last night, it was an easy decision to put me full-time on the murders and any possible linkage to Motts."

"That *is* good news."

"How's it going on your end?" she asked.

"I'm trying to find Sarah Elliott's case file on Motts," he replied. "But I've hit a roadblock. I can't locate her briefcase or find keys to her office file cabinet. They seem to have disappeared."

"And her law office partner can't help?"

"He hasn't so far, but I'll keep looking. The file has to be somewhere."

"I'll let you know if I find out anything from Grandma Motts later today."

"Okay. Stay safe."

FOWLER'S NEXT MOVE was to meet with Elliott at the city jail and press him on what he knew about Sarah's briefcase and office keys. But first he wanted to take another look around Elliott's home.

It was a warm fall afternoon on his drive to Stonefield Estates, and the sun coming through the windshield energized his sleep-deprived body. As he drove the winding route to Elliott's home, the streets were filled with golf carts and joggers. It seemed the unseasonably warm weather prompted many residents to play hooky.

Yellow crime tape was still draped over the entrance of the sprawling ranch home, warning everyone to stay away. Fowler ducked under the tape and opened the Elliotts' front door using his pass key.

The home was cool and quiet. Sunlight flooded through the wall of windows at the back of the living room, providing ample visibility down the hallway and into the house.

Fowler knew another search would likely be futile. Something as large as a briefcase would have had to be found on the earlier searches.

He opened the doors to the two closets off the hallway, looking above and below the coats and jackets that hung inside. He checked each coat pocket for keys, but only found gum wrappers and receipts, mostly for gasoline.

Over the next thirty minutes, he pulled out every drawer in the kitchen and opened every cabinet in the living room and den. There was no sign of a briefcase or keys.

Finally, he moved to the master bedroom.

An attempt had been made to clean the room. Faded bloodstains remained on the carpet at the foot of the large bed.

The smell of bleach stung his nostrils as he entered the en suite bathroom. The room was spotless. Every item had been returned to its proper place. He found no keys in the cabinets or drawers.

The master closet was as big as most normal bedrooms and remained filled with hanging clothes--Sarah's on the right, Rand's on the left. Fowler pushed items aside as he searched, but he found nothing. He checked the pockets of sport coats and suit coats on both sides of the massive closet. He found no keys, but did find a receipt in the pocket of one of Sarah's jackets.

The receipt was from the Vista View Inn restaurant in Asheville. It was dated two weeks ago in the amount of $175.50 and included a $50.00 bottle of Vista View wine and what appeared to be two meals. He stuffed the small paper into his pants pocket and headed back toward the front porch.

As expected, the search provided nothing more than peace of mind that Sarah's keys and briefcase had not been overlooked. They clearly were not there.

As he locked the door behind him and stepped off the porch, a jogger in blue nylon pants and long-sleeved turtleneck slowed to a walk.

"Hey, Detective," the dark-haired man called out.

It took a second, but Fowler finally attached a name to the face.

"Dr. Felton, you're taking the day off I assume."

"After twenty-five years of practice, I only work three days a week now," he said. "It's a pretty good gig."

"I'll never know," Fowler replied. "The lucky cops grow old on the job."

"So, what brings you back here?" Felton asked. "I thought you had your guy."

"There are always loose ends to tie up. This case is no different."

"Loose ends? I hear you found the murder weapon. What more do you need?"

"I can't really comment, but it's fair to say there are always unanswered questions."

Felton frowned.

"Well, everyone around here hoped the case was solved," he said. "No one wants to think there's a murderer still out there."

"I wouldn't spend much time worrying about that," Fowler said, slowly moving toward his car. "My colleagues and I worry enough for everyone."

"I'm sure," Felton replied.

"Do you still have my card in case anything comes up?" Fowler asked, reaching for his car door.

"Yeah, but I doubt if anything will."

"Take care," Fowler said before stepping into his car and slowly pulling away.

- 5.3 -

IN A LAVISH OFFICE COMPLEX near a spaghetti-like interchange in south Charlotte, Erik Rolland, the CEO of Cap INC, was in conference with his chief of operations, Jerald Jefferson.

They were meeting in Rolland's private office which was the size of a hotel lobby located on the top floor of a shimmering eight-story glass building. The muscular former longshoreman with a gleaming shaved head sat behind his massive desk. His suit coat was removed to reveal an $80 tie and starched white shirt, stretching at the chest and biceps. Dark, caterpillar-like eyebrows were perched over his steel blue eyes that moved up and down in unison as he berated the man seated before him.

"J.J, you have one damned job to do," he shouted. "I assume you know what it is."

"Yes, sir," he answered.

The handsome, clean-shaven black man dressed in a pin-striped suit held a black belt in karate, multiple business degrees, and past jobs ranging from a nightclub bouncer to chief financial officer. He was hand-selected by Rolland, and Jefferson took the job for one reason only—to become wealthy.

"It's taken me two decades to work my way from the streets to this position," Rolland bellowed, "and I've never had so many pissants snooping into my business as I've had lately. It's your job to make sure the pissants stay away."

"I understand."

"It wasn't that easy. The state's been cracking down on trafficking, and the DA was making an example with Motts. He was attempting to get him to plea bargain, pressuring him to provide damaging information on Cap INC."

"Did he?"

"Motts knew his life wouldn't be worth two cents if he talked. To be safe, I decided it would be best if he was out of the way."

"You took him out?"

"Yeah. But now the SBI in Charlotte is asking questions about Motts and MedEX. We had to clean up a little problem with a couple informants the other day."

"What about Motts' attorney? Was that part of your cleanup?"

"She was recommended by one of our associates to defend Motts, but her death wasn't anything we directed. Frankly, I don't know what happened. She would have been a loose end for us to deal with, but she was already dead before we had to do anything."

"I trust that's the end of the Motts saga."

"Not exactly. There's one more thing," Jefferson said.

"Not more," Rolland groaned, pulling his hand over his bald dome.

"Motts was heading up the plan to add fentanyl to our generic pain pills sold under the MedEX brand," Jefferson said.

"Get someone else to lead it," Rolland barked. "That drug brings in millions, and so far, it's passing for legit."

"And that's the problem. Adding fentanyl will put the pills beyond legal limits. The change in formula could also increase the number of fatal overdoses from the drug."

"I thought our goal was to increase dependency, not kill people," Rolland said.

"There's a balance between establishing higher dependency and the risk of increasing overdoses," Jefferson replied.

"And when is this change in the formula planned?"

"Production was to start early next week, distribution to begin as soon as we get supply built," Jefferson replied. "We're still on that schedule unless you decide to change it."

Rolland paused.

"Move forward with the schedule."

Jefferson smiled.

"Good. I've already set up Motts as the fall guy if we experience any blowback on the fentanyl content."

"Now getting back to Motts," Rolland said, brushing aside the previous discussion. "The way that situation was handled snowballed out of control. Make sure the Motts mess has been cleaned up. And that includes removing anyone who continues to snoop into our business."

"Yes, sir. Consider it done."

- 5.4 -

DETECTIVE JONES WAS UNABLE to reach Jasmine Motts on the phone, so she drove unannounced to the North Davidson (NoDa) address she'd found in Motts' police file.

From the outside, the townhome complex where Mrs. Motts lived appeared pristine. The homes were freshly painted, the shrubbery was manicured, and there wasn't a hint of clutter anywhere.

The location was ideal. Nearby dining was among the best in the Queen City and high-end shopping was a walk or short Uber drive away. Townhomes in the NoDa district, similar to those in Jasmine Motts' development, sold in the range of $500K to over one million. It was clear Malone Motts' grandmother was living well.

Knowing she had a 35-year-old grandson, Jones estimated Jasmine Motts to be in her early to mid-80s, but the woman who came to the door of the two-story unit appeared much younger.

Mrs. Motts' smile was natural and contagious. She was stylishly dressed in a red tunic and brightly colored slacks, with her snow-white hair coiled atop her head.

"I'm Detective Angela Jones. I apologize for coming unannounced, but I was unable to reach you by phone. Are you Mrs. Motts?"

"Yes. Is this about my grandson?" she asked, her smile melting.

"Yes. And let me say how sorry I am for your loss."

"It seemed he'd been doing so well. His death was a total shock," she said, her bottom lip beginning to tremble.

"May I come in and ask you some questions about your grandson? I won't take more than ten minutes of your time."

"Sure. Let's sit in the kitchen. I was just having my afternoon tea."

She led Jones down a hallway toward the back of the bright and spacious townhome.

"You have a lovely place, Mrs. Motts."

"Thanks, and everyone calls me Jazz, short for Jasmine," she replied. "It makes me feel young."

"Sure, and you can call me Angela."

Mrs. Motts held up an empty tea cup toward Jones.

"No tea for me. Thanks," Jones said, taking a seat at the table across from Mrs. Motts. "When was the last time you talked with Malone?"

"Only once after he was arrested. I lose track of time, but I think it was about ten days ago."

"What did you talk about?"

"He wanted me to know everything would be okay, and that his arrest was a mistake. He said someone else placed the drugs in his trunk, and he would be free soon."

"Your grandson thought he'd been framed?"

"Yes."

"Did he know who set him up?"

"He didn't say."

"Did your grandson ever mention his defense attorney, Sarah Elliott?"

"Yes, he seemed pleased that she was helping him."

"Did he ever mention that he or his attorney had enemies, people who wished to harm them?"

"No. Never. I was shocked when I heard what her husband had done to that poor woman," Mrs. Motts replied. "You just never know about people, do you?"

"Did your grandson ever discuss his work with you?"

"Not a lot," she replied, "but it seemed he was excited about what he was doing. He said he ran a pharmaceutical company. He had a degree in business, you know."

"Yes, I'm aware."

"It took Malone several years to get his life together after my son and daughter-in-law were killed in that dreadful crash, but he was finally doing well."

"Did Malone ever seem depressed, or were you ever concerned with his emotional stability?"

"Sure, after losing his parents, but not recently. Not for at least the past five years. He seemed to have everything going in the right direction."

"So, you must've been shocked that he died from an overdose," Jones asked.

"He hadn't used drugs in years!" Mrs. Motts bristled. "There's no way he knowingly took those drugs."

"What do you think happened?"

"There are bad people inside prisons. One of them must've killed my grandson. He was poisoned. I called the people at the Asheville courthouse and told them that, but they didn't listen. They treated me like I was some old fuddy-duddy."

"I'm sorry to hear that, Mrs. Motts. I mean Jazz."

"I didn't see Malone that often, but I know he loved his grandma," she said softly as tears escaped down her cheek. "He called me on my birthday and at Christmas. And he never asked me for money, not even years ago when I know he needed it."

Mrs. Motts paused and took a deep breath, patting her eyes with a napkin.

"If I may ask a final question," Jones said. "What did you and your husband do for a living?"

"Fred was a commercial builder. He had a degree in civil engineering. I was a part-time dancer and actor, mostly off Broadway and on Charlotte stages," she replied, her face springing back to life.

"I can see you as a dancer," Jones said, smiling. "You carry yourself gracefully."

"Thank you. I may have never been as pretty as you," Mrs. Motts said, "but I could still turn a few heads in my day."

Jones stood and pushed her chair back to the table.

"You've been gracious with your time, Jazz. Thank you."

"Come back anytime. I don't get many visitors," she said, walking Jones to the front door.

ON HER DRIVE HOME, Jones called Fowler and gave him an update on what she'd learned from Motts' grandmother.

"It doesn't sound like Motts had a reason for killing his attorney," Fowler said.

"Nor does it seem like Motts was a user or had any reason to kill himself," Jones added. "I didn't expect his grandmother to know much about his job, so I didn't learn much about Motts' business associates."

"Even if there was turmoil at his work, I wouldn't think he'd share that information with his grandmother," Fowler said.

"How'd *you* do today?" Jones asked.

"I wasn't able to get with Elliott, but I did stop by and talk with Watkins about getting access to Motts' case file."

"What did he say?"

"He said even if he had the file, he couldn't release it. The information remains protected by the attorney-client privilege."

"For crying out loud, the attorney and the client are both dead. Doesn't he realize that?"

"He claims it doesn't matter, and it will take a court order to have the file released. But first we have to find it," he said. "There's no sign of the file. The keys to Sarah Elliott's file cabinet are missing and so is her briefcase."

"The CSI team didn't find them?"

"No, and I spent over an hour at the Elliott house today to make sure they weren't there."

"Why couldn't you get with Elliott today?" she asked.

"Watkins had him tied up most of the day, and then when I went to meet with him, Elliott said he wasn't feeling well. Blamed it on bad food."

"Sounds like he didn't want to explain why he lied about his alibi," Jones said.

"Probably, but I'll get to him tomorrow morning."

"I keep wondering what those two guys were going to tell me that got them killed."

"It could be the same information that got Motts killed," Fowler replied. "And I have a bad feeling that if we don't soon figure out what they had to say, those three men won't be the only casualties."

- DAY 6 -

Wednesday

WITH DETECTIVE JENKINS STILL at home with the flu, Fowler pushed forward on his own with the murder investigation. He called Watkins and demanded to speak with Elliott.

"I'm not buying your client's story about food poisoning," Fowler told Watkins. "I need to speak with Elliott this morning."

"I have a pre-trial hearing that should be over by ten," Watkins replied.

"No more delays," Fowler insisted. "I'll meet you at the police station at ten sharp!"

AT FOWLER'S REQUEST, the jailer removed Elliott from his cell and led him toward the interrogation room inside the police station.

Fowler stepped from the detectives' bullpen and spotted Elliott shuffling down the hall in an ill-fitting, orange jumpsuit. In contrast to his prior appearance, he was looking more like a hardened prisoner. His sandy hair was uncombed and matted to his head. Dark circles had formed under his eyes and his face was covered with a brown stubble that looked more like dirt than a beard.

"Where's Watkins?" Elliott barked as Fowler approached.

"He was supposed to be here at ten," Fowler replied. "We can start without him if you want."

"No chance. I'll wait," he snapped. "I'm in no hurry to get back to that hellhole."

"You're not going to do well in prison. Our city jail is a resort compared to federal lockups."

The tall, angular jailer pulled out a chair from the small metal table and pressed his prisoner onto it. He then stepped outside and stood guard near the door. Fowler remained standing across from Elliott as he waited for Watkins.

"What's so bad about our facility?" Fowler asked, filling the awkward silence.

"The drunk they threw in the cell next to me at two a.m. smelled like rotting potatoes, and he wouldn't shut up," Elliott whined.

"That's unusual. The drunks usually come in on Saturday night. I'll talk to the jailer about your neighbors."

"I'd appreciate it."

"I got here as fast as I could," Watkins said, breathing heavily as he hurried into the room. "The parking lot was full, so I had to park down the street."

"You didn't miss anything," Fowler said, taking a seat next to Elliott. "Your client was just commenting on his accommodations."

"Go ahead. Let's get started," Watkins said. "I have a busy day."

Fowler leaned close to Elliott with a piercing stare.

"Why don't we start with you telling me the truth about what you did after leaving Fool's Gold on Friday night. We have a witness who saw you depart before seven."

Elliott took a deep breath and glanced at Watkins before speaking.

"I took a leak before leaving and then talked with one of the waitresses for a couple minutes near the entrance. Jane, I think her name is. I'm sure it was well after seven before I was in my car."

Fowler rolled his eyes.

"Go on," he urged.

"I remember the traffic was still pretty heavy with commuters--stop and go for a while. It probably took me around an hour and a half to get home."

"So, are you now saying you arrived at eight-thirty?"

"No, I'm sure it was closer to nine. I arrived just a few minutes before I called nine-one-one."

"It seems you could've easily arrived by eight if you left at seven. It's less than sixty miles door-to-door. I measured it," Fowler argued, his brow furrowed.

"Someone must've seen my Tesla drive through the neighborhood," Elliott pleaded.

"Sarah's briefcase and office keys are missing," Fowler said, changing gears. "Do you have any idea where they are?"

"Like I told my attorney, Sarah always set her briefcase in the front hall closet. Her office keys were snapped on a loop inside the case. She rarely worked at home, and she put the briefcase in the closet so she didn't have to look for it when she headed back to the office."

"So, where is it now?"

"I have no idea. I guess whoever killed her took it for some reason," Elliott replied.

"Is this your final story, or will it continue to evolve?" Fowler asked.

"Enough with the sarcasm," Watkins said, raising his voice. "My client's been cooperative from the beginning. Now, if you don't have anything else, I should be on my way."

"There is one more thing," Fowler said, lifting a narrow slip of paper from his sport coat. "I found this inside the pocket of your wife's jacket hanging in your closet."

"You haven't shared this with me," Watkins said, bending forward and squinting his eyes to read the paper. "What is it?"

"It's a receipt from the Vista View Inn restaurant dated ten days ago. The total is more than a hundred and seventy-five bucks, and it includes a fifty-dollar bottle of wine, a steak, and an order of lasagna."

Fowler stared at Elliott, waiting for a reaction. He didn't get one.

"What's your point?" Elliott asked. "She's an attorney. She was probably meeting with a client."

"The tab was charged to a room," Fowler said. "I already checked it out. The name on the room register was Elle Dearing. I'll make a wild guess and say your wife was hiding her identity for some reason."

Elliott froze.

"Is it possible you learned of your wife's out-of-town liaisons, and the news pushed you over the edge last Friday night?"

"Fowler, you're way out in front of your headlights," Watkins said. "It may be as simple as Sarah wanted some time alone—away from the pressure of the courtroom."

"Right. And she must've been very hungry and thirsty," Fowler mocked. "It should be easy to verify if she was alone. I'll put Jenkins on it as soon as he's back."

"I'm out of time," Watkins said, standing. "Let me know what you find out."

Fowler gave Elliott one final stare before standing and stepping out the door.

"You can take him back to his cell," Fowler told the jailer. "And FYI, he really enjoys having company in the cell next door."

- 6.1 -

CHIEF PIERCE WAS SUMMONED to the mayor's office for an afternoon meeting. Pierce was away when Mayor Willis called, so the chief's new assistant, Brad Visser, absorbed the initial salvo from the angry city leader. The young officer was unfamiliar with the status of the Elliott murder investigation, so the mayor's probing questions went unanswered.

Furious, the round-faced, stocky politician signed off with his bulbous neck the same color as his crimson tie.

"Make sure Chief Pierce and Detective Fowler are in my office at two p.m. sharp, or there'll be hell to pay!"

PIERCE AND FOWLER arrived at city hall a few minutes early, giving the mayor one less thing to fume about.

Aware of the pending confrontation, Willis' assistant silently directed the men inside the mayor's office with a finger point, barely looking up as they passed.

Inside, the DA, Ron Olsen, sat smugly in a leather chair beside the mayor's desk. In his ever-present three-piece suit, Willis sat atop his desk chair, raised to where his stubby legs barely touched the ground.

Willis' bulldog, Rocky, was sprawled out on a deep cushion in the corner of the room. The dog, which had a strong resemblance to the mayor, had become a fixture in the office over the years. Rocky raised his bulky head when Pierce and

Fowler entered, but the aging canine quickly resumed a resting position.

"Have a seat, gentlemen," Willis said. "This could take a while."

"I assume by Mr. Olsen's presence this has to do with the Elliott murder investigation," Pierce said.

Neither Olsen nor Willis responded, ignoring the question.

"Have you been reading the papers and watching the local news stations, Chief?" Willis asked.

"When I have time," Pierce replied.

"Well, I suggest you make the time!" he bellowed. "Our community remains on edge. The citizens are taking less and less comfort in the fact that Rand Elliott is behind bars, charged with the murder of his wife. And you know why?"

"I'm sure you're going to tell me, " Pierce replied.

"Because the press is fascinated with the possibility that organized crime may have played a role in Sarah Elliott's murder. That's why."

Pierce leaned forward in his chair, staring at the mayor.

"I can assure you neither I nor anyone on my force has said one word to the press about Malone Motts' death or the murders of the two men in Charlotte," Pierce argued. "All that talk comes from the Charlotte media. If anything, I've been clear in my press briefings that we have the evidence to arrest and try Rand Elliott for the murder of his wife."

"Then why in the hell are you having your detective spend time looking for Sarah Elliott's file on Motts?" Olsen interjected. "You can't be searching for more evidence against Rand Elliott in *that* file."

"I'd think any DA worth his salt would be curious what might be in the file," Fowler shot back. "Or is it best to have tunnel vision when looking for leads to a murder?"

"I have what I need to prosecute and convict Rand Elliott," Olsen argued. "All you're doing is creating doubt for his defense."

"And you don't think his attorney is capable of doing the same thing?" Fowler asked. "Best to have facts going into the trial than to have them thrown in your face in front of the judge and jury."

"And that's what they taught you at Piedmont Community College?" Olsen sneered.

Fowler rose from his seat and took a step toward Olsen.

"Sit down!" Pierce shouted.

Fowler paused before slowly taking a seat.

"Good boy," Olsen said under his breath, drawing a warning stare from Pierce.

"I fear for the prosecution of justice in this district if our DA resorts to petty personal attacks as his first instinct," Pierce said.

Olsen failed to find words for a comeback.

"Everyone take a breath," Willis said, leaning forward with his forearms pressed to his desk. "Our mutual objective is to provide a safe and secure town, and have the residents confident in their community leaders and law enforcement."

"What would you have me do differently, Mayor?" Pierce asked.

"Keep within your jurisdiction and stop meeting with the defense attorney," Olsen interrupted.

"The chief was talking to me," Willis said, shooting a stare at the young DA.

"We all need to show confidence that we've arrested the right man," Willis said. "To that end, I'd like you and me to host a joint press conference where we say just that and put an end to the speculation of other murderers being out there."

"We can't bury our heads in the sand," Fowler said. "There's more than a reasonable doubt that others could have been involved in Sarah Elliott's death."

"Show me the evidence," Willis barked. "I'm aware that Sarah Elliott was defending a dangerous man who was surrounded by dangerous men, but I've neither seen nor heard of any solid evidence they were involved in her death."

"So, we just sit on what we have?" Fowler asked.

"Let law enforcement in the jurisdictions where these suspects reside and committed their crimes prove what you only suspect," Willis said.

"Police departments share information across neighboring jurisdictions all the time. You're not suggesting we put up walls between us and adjacent law enforcement agencies, are you?" Pierce asked.

"Let the SBI and local Asheville and Charlotte police lead the investigations into Motts and these crime rings," Willis replied. "Your force isn't big enough to protect the entire state."

Fowler started to respond, but Pierce raised his hand and cut him off.

"I'll agree to the joint press meeting, and we'll do our best on your other requests," Pierce said.

"They aren't requests, Chief," Willis said, standing.

"Are we done here?" Pierce asked.

Willis nodded.

Pierce and Fowler rose and marched out.

STANDING BESIDE Pierce's parked car, Fowler's lips were pressed thin. He'd waited until they were clear of the mayor's office before he blew.

"We both know that all those two pinheads care about is public opinion and getting re-elected," Fowler erupted. "They don't give a shit about justice or what it takes to achieve it."

"Be careful, Jack. That's my boss you're talking about. You may be right about Olsen, but I've known Mayor Willis long enough to know he cares about this town."

"You can't possibly agree with stopping our investigations at the city limits."

"No, but when we venture outside of town, we need to make sure local law enforcement is aware we're there. And better yet, they should be alongside of us."

"I'm glad to hear you say that," Fowler replied. "I have a call in Asheville tomorrow to follow up on Sarah Elliott's activities at the Vista View Inn. And then I plan on swinging by the county jail. The sheriff has arranged for me to meet with two prisoners who were housed near Motts during his lockup."

"Try not to draw attention to your trip," Pierce said. "For crying out loud, keep a low profile."

"As always," Fowler replied, before both men stepped inside the car.

"Have you heard anything from Jenkins?" Fowler asked. "I could use the company on the drive over."

"His wife called around noon and said he was getting worse, and if his breathing doesn't improve, he may need to be hospitalized."

"Damn. That doesn't sound good," Fowler said. "He looked healthier than me when we were in Charlotte a few days ago."

"You'll have to go it alone for now," Pierce said. "I've got no one available."

BACK AT HIS DESK, Fowler grabbed his cellphone and called Detective Jones. She answered in her car.

"How's it going?" she asked.

"Pierce and I just had a meeting with the mayor and the DA," Fowler said. "To say it was heated would be an understatement."

"What happened?"

"It's a long story, but in a nutshell, Ron Olsen is pissed that we aren't closing the case on the Elliott murder and just letting him go to trial. Mayor Willis is upset that the town is on edge, and says we're giving the impression murderers are still out there by continuing our investigation."

"What pinheads!"

"That's exactly what I said to Pierce."

"I made some progress with the IRS agent who's auditing Cap INC," Jones said. "He didn't want to talk on the phone and suggested we meet tomorrow with the FBI agent assigned to the case."

"Sounds like tomorrow could be moving day on our investigations," Fowler said. "I'll be in Asheville digging around at the Vista View Inn and then I'll head to the jail to talk with inmates who may've spoken with Motts."

"I wish we could partner up," Jones said. "Lieutenant Alvarez is working to assign someone to me now that I'm officially off that task force."

"And it doesn't sound like Jenkins is coming back anytime soon. Pierce just told me if he gets worse, he may need to be admitted to the hospital."

"I really hate to hear that," Jones said.

"Can't you hold your boss off from assigning a partner until we can determine if Motts and Cap INC are linked to the Elliott murder?" Fowler asked. "Willis and Olsen will have kittens if I work the Cap INC investigation before a connection in the cases can be made."

"I'll talk to Alvarez, but he's a little worried about me going alone on a case involving a double homicide," Jones said. "I told him no need to concern himself. What is it with you men, anyway?"

"I'll assume that was a rhetorical question."

"Let's connect late tomorrow to compare notes," Jones said.

"Sounds good. Be safe."

- DAY 7 -

Thursday

FOWLER'S MIND WANDERED during the early morning drive to Asheville. The hills of Stonefield quickly grew into mountains during the 90-minute trip west. It was hard not to be distracted by the layered mountaintops. Ridge after ridge rose through low-hanging clouds, each outdoing the next with increasing panoramic color.

On these trips, he missed having a partner to keep him alert. To his surprise, he and Jenkins seemed to have a lot in common. He felt a little guilty that Jenkins' illness might give him a chance to work with Detective Jones, but given the opportunity, he wouldn't pass it up.

Fowler had prepared notes for his scheduled interviews. As he drove, he cycled through the questions, wondering if there was something he might have left out.

Following Chief Pierce's orders, Fowler had called the Asheville Police Department (APD) late yesterday afternoon and talked to the officer on duty. He informed the officer he would be in town investigating a murder and it was his intent to interview management and staff at the Vista View Inn as well as inmates at the Buncombe County Jail.

The officer on duty signed off by saying, "If you experience any situations requiring our support, call back to this number immediately."

ROAD SIGNS to the Vista View Inn and Resort directed Fowler off I-40 before reaching the city limits of Asheville. He wound around suburban roads until seeing the inn rising several stories in the distance.

The Vista View Inn was located ten miles from the center of Asheville on 300 acres of wooded property with 180-degree, long-range mountain views. Architects of the inn made a masterful attempt to recreate the stately elegance of the Vanderbilt mansion located a short drive away. Utilizing a combination of stone, steel, and rough-sawn logs in the exterior construction, the 25-year-old inn looked as if it could've been built in the 1800s.

Drawing closer, the grounds surrounding the inn were vast and impeccably kept. Not a blade of grass appeared out of place. The leaves that had fallen must've been instantly sucked up and whisked away, leaving an undisturbed green carpet behind.

Fowler drove past wide-eyed attendants at a valet stand just outside the grand entrance to the inn. Wearing matching red vests, the young attendants stared at the large grey vehicle as it lumbered toward the nearest parking lot. Fowler pulled in one space away from handicap parking, grabbed his notepad, and stepped out.

He could hear the attendants poking fun at his car as he approached the entrance.

Keep a low profile, he reminded himself.

Even with Chief Pierce's warning fresh in his mind, Fowler couldn't resist.

He pulled his badge from his breast pocket as he stepped toward three young men gathered at the valet stand. Their banter subsided, but grins remained plastered on their faces.

"I'm Detective Fowler, and I'll be here for an hour or so this morning," he said, extending his badge to the face of the tallest attendant.

"Is there something wrong?" the lanky youth asked, his grin vanishing.

"No, everything's just fine, but I was wondering if you could keep an eye on my car over there," he said, pointing to the Grey Ghost. "Ordinarily I'd valet park it, but it's a registered police vehicle, and I'm particular about who drives it."

The three young men turned in unison and stared at Fowler's car.

"Sure, we'll keep an eye on it," the taller attendant replied.

"Great," Fowler said, pulling his jacket back far enough to give the attendants a glimpse of his holster as he stuffed his badge back into his pocket. "You all have a good morning."

He turned and stepped toward the entrance, leaving the young men standing in silence.

The expansive lobby of the inn reeked of opulence with 30-foot-high vaulted ceilings, expensive furnishings, and crystal chandeliers. It didn't strike Fowler as the kind of place a small-time defense attorney would select to meet clients for dinner, much less have a sufficient expense account to stay there. It was near check-out time, and the lobby was bustling with guests making their ways to taxis and rental cars.

He approached a glossy-topped information counter staffed by two attractive young ladies, both wearing tailored gold tweed jackets displaying the Vista View seal over the breast pocket.

"How may I help you?" the shorter of the two women asked with a broad smile. *Jennifer* was printed on her name tag.

"I'm Detective Jack Fowler, and I'm here to meet with your concierge manager, Ms. Miller."

"Is she expecting you?" the brown-eyed woman asked, continuing to smile.

"Yes, I have a ten o'clock appointment."

Jennifer picked up the receiver from a phone behind the counter and tapped in three numbers.

"A Detective Fowler is here to see you."

The response on the other end was brief. She quickly returned the receiver to the phone.

"Ms. Miller's office is to the right of the check-in counter," she said, pointing across the lobby. "Her name is beside her door. She said for you to come on in."

Fowler turned and stepped briskly toward the far end of the lobby. A petite blonde woman in her 40s dressed in a dark blue pantsuit was waiting outside Ms. Miller's office door.

"Detective Fowler, I assume?" she greeted. "I'm Sharon Miller. Please come on in."

Her office was well-appointed but modest by the hotel's standards.

"Can I have someone get you something to drink? And maybe one of our cookies? They're baked fresh each morning," she said, pointing Fowler to a chair across from her desk.

"No thanks," Fowler replied, sitting.

"I understand you have questions about one of our guests."

"That's right. I'm trying to trace the activities of Sarah Elliott during the days prior to her murder."

"Oh, my!" Miller gasped, covering her mouth. "I had no idea."

"We found a receipt from your hotel restaurant in her coat pocket dated two weeks ago," Fowler continued. "And based on the items on the receipt, it appears she may have dined with someone that night."

He placed the receipt on the desk in front of the hotel manager. She picked it up and read it quickly before placing it back on her desk.

"This does appear to be a receipt from our restaurant, charged to room three sixteen."

"We've checked your records for the room on that night, and it was registered to Elle Dearing. We have reason to believe Mrs. Elliott was using a fake name, but your clerk will not release the name of the guest who paid."

"We allow guests to register under false names as long as they provide proof of identity when checking in. We respect their right to privacy, but we obviously need to know who's staying at our hotel."

"I need to find out who Sarah Elliott may have been with that evening."

"We don't make a practice of providing private information about our guests," Miller replied.

Fowler took a deep breath before placing his detective badge faceup on Miller's desk. She stared at the badge before looking back at Fowler.

"Ms. Miller, time is precious in a murder investigation. I can contact a judge, and in a few days, get a court order to release this information. Or you can have someone go to a computer right now and provide what I'm asking by typing a few keystrokes."

Miller thought as she stared down at the receipt on her desk.

"You say this woman has been murdered?" she asked.

"That's correct."

"Then I see no reason for you to wait."

Miller picked up her phone.

"Have Dave step in my office," she said.

Seconds later a young man with short dark hair, wearing the same gold jacket as the women at the information desk, stepped into the office.

"Dave, find out the name of the person who registered and paid for room three sixteen on the day of this receipt."

"And would it be possible to determine who on your staff checked them in as well as who their restaurant server was that night?" Fowler asked.

"I guess we can provide that," she replied. "Dave, please get that information, too."

"Will do," he said, stepping out of the office with the receipt in hand.

"This should only take a few minutes," Miller said. "Is there anything else I can help with while we wait?"

Fowler reached into his coat pocket, pulled out a 3x5-inch photo of Sarah Elliott, and handed it to Miller.

"I was hoping whoever waited on Sarah that night might recognize her from this picture and be able to describe who she was with."

Miller looked at the photo for several seconds, and then handed it back.

"I can't say that I've seen her before, but then I interact with hundreds of guests each week," she said. "Do you think she may have been with the person who killed her that night?"

"I can't say," Fowler replied. "But knowing who she was with could be key evidence in the case."

A few minutes later, Dave hurried back into the room.

"What did you find out?" Miller asked.

"Ms. Elle Dearing provided a driver's license at check-in. Her name is on the room register for that night," he replied. "She paid cash at check-in for one night and then settled up in cash at checkout."

"Elle Dearing? You're sure?" Fowler asked.

"Yes, I double-checked."

"Do you have a copy of her driver's license on file?"

"No. We don't keep that information after checkout."

Fowler turned to Miller.

"Paying with cash is rare, isn't it?" he asked.

"Yes. We have very few cash transactions."

"Sounds to me like something the desk clerks would remember," Fowler said.

"Debbie checked her in," the young clerk said, "but she doesn't come in until this later this afternoon. Same with Vincent, who waited on Ms. Dearing in the dining room that night. He works the late shift."

"What about the desk clerk who checked her out?" Fowler asked.

"Tom Brown checked her out," Dave replied. "He's working this morning, but I didn't know if you wanted me to say anything to him."

"Have him come in," Miller said. "Relieve him at his station if he's busy."

A moment later, a tall, thin man with light hair entered the office appearing barely old enough to shave.

"Tom, this gentleman is Detective Fowler from the Stonefield Police Department. He's looking for information on this woman who stayed here about two weeks ago," Miller said, handing Tom the photo. "You checked her out and she paid in cash. Do you remember her?"

"Yeah, sure. I remember," Tom replied. "I thought it was unusual."

"Was she with anyone?" Fowler asked.

"I'm pretty sure she was with a gentleman, but he stood back as she paid. I didn't get a good look at him."

"Was he tall or short, thin or fat? Anything will help," Fowler said.

"I guess he was average height, taller than the blonde lady, anyway," Tom replied. "He had dark hair and was wearing a dark sport coat and grey slacks. That's about all I can remember."

"Did they leave together?"

"Yeah. They went directly out the entrance. They only had one bag and the woman carried it."

"Had you ever seen them here before?" Fowler asked.

"No. Not that I can remember."

Fowler paused.

"Is that all, Detective?" Miller asked.

"Yeah, that's all for now," he replied. "Thanks, Tom. You've been a big help."

"No problem," he said before stepping out the door.

"I'm on my way to another meeting," Fowler said, standing. "But I'll leave my card and this photo to show to the employees who come in later. Hopefully they can provide more details about the man she was with."

"I'll make sure they see it as soon as they arrive."

- 7.1 -

THE BUNCOMBE COUNTY JAIL in Asheville housed more than 500 inmates charged with a variety of crimes, mostly non-violent. Many inmates, like Malone Motts, were awaiting trial and were held in a common area of the facility.

Sometimes referred to as a detention center, the jail had a spotless record and was frequently cited as a model for similar centers. It was a relatively new, modern facility, deploying state-of-the-art processes and technology to ensure a safe and efficient environment. It seemed suspicious to Fowler that Malone Motts could find a way to overdose while housed there.

Sheriff Abbott had arranged for Ricky Alcott and Desmond Leaks to meet with Fowler. Both were three-time offenders, awaiting trial for drug-related charges. Alcott and Leaks shared the same court-appointed attorney, Cicely Washington. She would be present at both interviews.

A sheriff's deputy brought Ricky Alcott into a small room usually used by attorneys to meet with their clients. Fowler had been waiting inside for several minutes. Washington had yet to arrive.

The deputy sat Alcott, wearing a blue jumpsuit and handcuffs, in a chair across from Fowler. The lanky, white middle-aged man with strings of hair swept over his bald head had dark, deep-set eyes, red rashes on his face and arms, and a greyish complexion. Fowler had seen meth addicts before and Alcott fit the description.

A short time later, Alcott's attorney entered. Cicely Washington was a well-dressed, heavyset black woman. She had a pleasant face, but failed to smile when Fowler stood to introduce himself.

"Please stay seated," she said. "I have four other clients to see while I'm here, and I'm hoping this won't take long."

She plopped her briefcase on the table and sat as the deputy stepped outside and closed the door.

"Let's get started."

"I understand you were housed in a cell next to Malone Motts while he was here," Fowler began, turning to the strung-out looking inmate.

"Yeah. That's right."

"Did you ever speak with Motts?"

"Not really. He was an uppity black fella. Talked like a teacher."

"Did he ever mention his attorney, Sarah Elliott?"

"Nope."

"What about his work? Did he ever talk to you about his work?"

"Nope."

"Have you ever heard anyone inside this jail talk about getting access to drugs?" Fowler asked.

"I hope you're not asking my client if he's doing drugs inside this facility," Washington bristled.

"No, it's a general question. I'm just wondering if he's aware drugs are available," Fowler said.

"If you got money and friends, you can get anythin', anywhere," Alcott replied.

"I'm not sure Mr. Alcott has anything of interest to share," Fowler said, turning to Ms. Washington. "Could we move to your next client?"

"That's it? You brung me down here just fir that?" Alcott whined.

Washington stood and opened the door.

"We're ready for Desmond," she said.

The deputy took Alcott back to his cell, and returned a few minutes later with Desmond Leaks, a large black man with a shaved head and a penetrating scowl that seemed tattooed on his face. He studied Fowler as he sat.

"Desmond, this is Detective Fowler. He has a few questions for you. If there's anything you don't want to answer, that's up to you," Washington said.

"Mr. Leaks, did you …"

"Nobody calls me Mr. Leaks," he interrupted. "It's Dez or Desmond."

"Okay. Dez, did you speak with Malone Motts while he was housed next to you?"

"A little," he grunted.

"Did Motts talk to you about his work?"

"He told me he made drugs. Legal drugs. Said he ran the company."

"Did he mention why he was arrested?"

"Cops found fentanyl in his car. Surely, you know about that."

"Yes, I'm aware, but did he say how the fentanyl got there?"

"He just said it was all a mistake, but that's what we all say, isn't it?" he scoffed.

"Did he ever mention Cap INC?"

"No, but I know about Cap INC," Dez replied. "They're into a lot of shit--drugs, gambling, women."

"Have you ever worked with them?"

"Hold it right there, Detective," Washington said. "I thought we were here to discuss Malone Motts."

"Fair enough," Fowler replied. "Let me change the subject. Did Motts ever mention his attorney, Sarah Elliott?"

"He said she was killed--stabbed to death."

"Did he know who did it?"

"Detective, this sounds like information that might be worth something," Washington interrupted. "Are you able to offer my client a deal? He's here on his third trafficking arrest. He could use a good word to the DA."

"I don't represent the DA in this district, nor can I make an offer," Fowler replied. "But if your client provides information that helps close this case, I'll definitely put in a good word."

"Maybe we should wait until you speak to the DA," Washington said, pushing back from the table.

"I'm here now. I've got other leads I can follow. Any help I can provide your client goes away after I walk out that door."

She thought, staring at Fowler.

"Go ahead," she said. "Answer the question."

"Motts didn't know who killed his attorney," Dez replied. "He appeared to be shocked."

"We have reason to believe Motts and his employer MedEX are linked to Cap INC. From what you know about them, do you think they could've been involved in his attorney's death?"

"They're capable of killing anyone who gets in their way, Detective," Dez replied. "But the murder of the female attorney wasn't the work of professional killers--too messy and too many clues left behind."

Fowler paused, glancing at Washington, who appeared impressed with her client's feedback.

"Were you surprised when Motts was found dead in his cell soon after his attorney was killed?" Fowler asked.

"Sure. Why wouldn't I be?"

"Do you believe the coroner's report, saying it was an overdose?"

"It may have been an overdose, but it wasn't no suicide, or even accidental," Dez replied. "Motts didn't strike me as a user, and I can recognize a user. This guy told me he ran a drug company. If so, he wouldn't take something that could possibly kill him."

"So, what do you think happened to him?"

"Simple. Someone poisoned him."

"How?"

"Doesn't take much to lace food, candy, even chewing gum with enough fentanyl to kill you. It could've been done by any number of people."

"Has something like that happened in here before?" Fowler asked.

"I've never heard of it happening in here, but it wouldn't be the first time someone staged a hit on a prisoner," Dez replied.

"Do you have any idea who might've killed him?"

"Someone with money. A lot of people would've needed to be paid off, especially with the number of safeguards in this place."

"Detective, I really need to run," Washington said, standing. "I think Dez has been very cooperative, and I'll look forward to your call to the DA on his behalf."

"As soon as I get back to the station, I'll call," Fowler said. "Thanks for your time, Dez."

"Hey. Time is what I have plenty of."

Fowler walked with Cicely Washington through the winding complex toward the main entrance of the detention center.

"What's the deal with Dez?" Fowler asked. "He didn't strike me as a typical three-time offender."

"At one time, he was a promising pro football player," she replied. "He graduated from college and was offered a sizable signing bonus."

"What happened?"

"The money and the fame came too fast, and it left just as fast," she said. "He blew out a knee and was out of football before his first play as a pro. He was unable to deal with the blow to his career, and he got hooked up with the wrong crowd."

"Damn shame," Fowler said. "Seems like a bright guy."

"Don't forget the phone call," Washington said, peeling off from Fowler and walking down a corridor to her next meeting.

FOWLER CALLED PIERCE on his way back to Stonefield. He was at his desk.

It had already been a trying day for Chief Pierce, starting off with a joint press briefing alongside Mayor Willis, and moments ago he'd received a phone call from the hospital. Detective Jenkins had just been admitted suffering from pneumonia.

"What you got?" Pierce asked.

"Infidelity seems to run in the Elliott marriage," Fowler began. "A hotel desk clerk at the Vista View Inn says he saw a woman matching Sarah's description checking out ten days ago in the company of another man."

"Interesting."

"It gets better," Fowler continued. "She checked in using a fake driver's license with the name of Elle Dearing."

"The clerk was sure it was Sarah Elliott?" Pierce asked.

"Yes. I showed him her photo," he replied. "I'm still waiting to hear from the waiter who served Sarah and her guest at dinner the night before."

The desk chair groaned as Pierce leaned back and gazed up at the ceiling.

"This adds to Rand Elliott's motive," Pierce said. "Jealous husband kills cheating wife. It happens all the time."

"It's beginning to look that way. I also talked to an inmate who'd spoken with Motts. A guy named Desmond Leaks."

"Get anything credible?"

"He seemed to be on the level," Fowler replied. "His lawyer was looking for me to put in a good word with the DA, but he answered my questions not expecting anything in return."

"And?"

"And he doesn't think Motts committed suicide or knowingly took the drugs that killed him," Fowler replied. "He believes it was more likely Motts was poisoned."

"Did he have any idea who or how?"

"No, not really. Probably disguised in food," Fowler replied. "Motts never mentioned Cap INC to Leaks, but he'd heard of it. I asked if he thought Cap INC could be involved in either the Motts or Sarah Elliott deaths. He believed it was possible they were behind Motts' murder, but unlikely they killed Sarah Elliott."

"Why's that?"

"He said professional killers don't use knives—too messy and they leave clues."

"Doesn't sound like you found anything to rule out Rand Elliott as the killer or to connect the Malone Motts case to the Sarah Elliott murder."

"Not yet," Fowler replied. "But I'm hoping Detective Jones is able to uncover something new from the IRS."

There was a pause in the conversation as Fowler waited.

"Say, Jack," Pierce said.

"You never call me Jack unless it's something serious. What is it?"

"Jenkins is worse. He was admitted to the hospital with viral pneumonia," Pierce replied, tension in his voice. "I'm going to wrap up early and head over there."

"I don't know what to say," Fowler replied. "Let me know if there's anything I can do."

"I will."

- 7.2 -

THE CHARLOTTE FBI office was located a few miles southwest of the city near the outer loop. Those housed within served a multi-county area, including Mecklenburg. The five-story, rectangular cement structure with rows of dark narrow windows offered no prominent signage, but it didn't need to. The building looked like hundreds of other U.S. government facilities.

Detective Jones had arranged a meeting with FBI Special Agent Aaron Fox through a call with Sam Waterman from the IRS. Fox and Waterman were investigating tax fraud and money laundering charges against Cap INC, both federal offenses.

After going through a labyrinth of checkpoints and screenings, Detective Jones made her way to the 4th floor office of Agent Fox. She noticed most everyone in the building was dressed in dark suits, white shirts, and narrow ties. It was as if time had stood still inside the federal building with agents resembling Efrem Zimbalist, Jr. from the 1960s TV series, *The FBI.*

Agent Fox was a veteran of the force—early 50s, tall, fit with close-cropped hair and dark-rimmed glasses. He was seated at his desk with a narrow window to his rear overlooking a grassy field with I-485 in the distance.

As he stood to greet Jones, his eyes widened and a greasy smile spread across his face.

"I'm Detective Angela Jones. I'm here to meet with you and Agent Waterman."

"Good afternoon," he said, extending his hand. "I just had a call from Agent Waterman. He should be here shortly. Please have a seat."

Jones sat across from his desk as Fox settled back into his chair.

"I apologize if I appeared surprised," he said. "It's just that I don't get many visitors who look like you."

Her scowl was immediate.

"I don't know what to make of your comment," Jones said. "Would you care to explain?"

"It was intended as a compliment," he said, quickly backtracking. "You're very attractive. That's all I meant."

Jones continued to silently boil, pausing to collect herself.

An unease hung in the room as Agent Waterman entered. The balding, middle-aged man's tie was askew and his shirttail had come loose in the front. He appeared frazzled, looking like he'd just come from babysitting five-year-old triplets.

"Sorry I'm a little late, but my team's in the middle of a huge corporate audit that has somehow leaked to the press. As a heads-up, I may get a call requiring I step away."

With the attention turning to Waterman, Fox took a deep breath and regrouped.

"Sam, this is Detective Angela Jones. We were just getting started," he said. "Have a seat. Hopefully your team will get things cleaned up before you get back."

The IRS agent settled into a chair next to Jones.

"Your email to Sam and me said you were working a murder case you thought might be related to Cap INC," Fox said, putting the meeting's rough start behind him.

"That's right. I'm investigating the death of Malone Motts, who managed MedEX, a company I understand may have connections to Cap INC," Jones said. "The Motts case became more complex just recently. I had arranged to meet with two informants to gather info on Motts when they were gunned down at an intersection near our meeting spot."

"I read up on the case," Fox said. "How can we help?"

"I was hoping you might know more about Malone Motts and any connection he might have to Cap INC," she replied.

"MedEX Pharmaceuticals is a small manufacturer in Charlotte," Fox began. "They produce a generic opioid that meets the standards for prescription pain medications, similar to oxycodone."

"So, the company's legit?" Jones asked.

"The DEA and FDA haven't found any violations to date," Fox replied.

"Motts was arrested with five kilos of fentanyl in his car," Jones said. "Is fentanyl something allowed in prescribed opioids?"

"It depends on where the fentanyl is manufactured, the amount used, and the treatment prescribed," Fox said. "Illegal and deadly fentanyl has recently been pouring over the southern border from a number of countries—China, Mexico, and others. The deaths related to the influx of these illegal drugs are escalating at a staggering rate."

"So, what about the fentanyl found in Motts' car?" Jones asked.

"It was from Mexico," Fox replied. "The DEA had it tested and it was similar to a hundred kilo shipment seized earlier that week. It had the same packaging, markings, and chemical content. Our guess is the five kilos in Motts' car was planted."

"You think he was being framed?"

"It's just a guess, but yes," Fox replied. "Motts wasn't stupid enough to carry around illegal fentanyl, not when his company manufactures it legally."

"Have you been able to verify any connection between Motts' company and Cap INC?" Jones asked.

"Nothing definitive," Waterman replied. "But we suspect MedEX isn't accurately reporting the amount of pain meds being produced, and Cap INC may be helping hide their real production."

"How's that?" she asked.

"What MedEX sells to their legal distributors, such as national pharmacies, gets closely monitored and the revenue carefully reported," Waterman explained. "But we suspect the company doesn't account for a large percentage of its production that's secretly distributed and sold elsewhere."

"Let me guess. It ends up on the streets," she said.

"Yes, it's likely sold through organized crime rings. We suspect the money ends up in Cap INC's coffers where they launder the funds through other businesses."

"Sounds like it would be easy to track the drugs coming out of MedEX," Jones said. "Or at least trace the flow of the drugs back from the users to where the drugs were purchased."

"There are dozens and dozens of copycat manufacturers out there, making it nearly impossible to investigate and analyze each one. When we seize a drug appearing to come from MedEX, they can easily claim it's not theirs."

"Why not shut down all production and use of synthetic fentanyl?" Jones asked. "Make it illegal like heroin or cocaine."

"Sounds like a good idea, but it's more complicated than that," Fox said. "While fentanyl and other opioids have become widely misused and lead to tens of thousands of deaths each year, these drugs have medical purposes, such as the treatment of chronic and severe pain. Many cancer patients and others are dependent upon them."

"Sounds like an unsolvable situation," she said. "But it doesn't help with my investigation. From what you know, what do you think happened to Motts?"

"If I were to bet, which I don't," Fox said, "I'd guess Motts got crossways with his higher-ups, or maybe with an associate who had aspirations to take his job, but I couldn't prove either."

"It was worth a shot," Jones said, standing to leave.

Agent Fox extended his hand, saying, "If I can be of further assistance, let me know."

"I doubt we'll be seeing each other again," Jones said, ignoring his hand and abruptly leaving the office.

As Jones walked down the hall toward the elevator, Waterman turned to Fox.

"What was *that* all about?" Waterman asked.

"Nothing really. The detective and I got off on the wrong foot," Fox replied. "No big deal."

- 7.3 -

FOWLER DECIDED to drive straight home. Last time he called the police station, Chief Pierce was still away at the hospital checking on Jenkins.

He thought about going to Stonefield General to see how his partner was doing, but he didn't know Jenkins' wife, Abby, very well. Pierce was there, and he'd known the family for 25 years.

It was dark by the time Fowler pulled into his garage and shut the double-wide door behind him. The brick ranch had been Fowler's boyhood home. Since his parents' deaths, he'd modernized the kitchen and updated the aging bathrooms. Angela had added her personal touches to the living room and the landscaping, which had been neglected for years. But even with all the changes, Fowler could still feel the presence of his parents every time he entered. As long as he was on SPD's detective force, he would not leave the house. It was home.

He'd just removed his jacket and hung up his holster inside the closet when his cellphone chirped. It was an Asheville area code.

"This is Detective Fowler."

"This is Sharon Miller from the Vista View Inn and Resort, and I wanted to pass on what Vincent told me after I showed him the photo of Mrs. Elliott."

"Vincent is the waiter?" Fowler asked.

"Yes, and he remembers serving her that night."

"Was she with someone?"

"Vincent said she was with a man older than Mrs. Elliott, maybe in his early fifties. She was in a dress and the man was wearing a dark suit and tie."

"Could he describe the man?"

"Only that he was older, average build, and had short dark hair. He did say that he assumed they were a couple, maybe on a date, and he was surprised when she signed the tab to her room."

"Thanks for getting back to me so quickly," Fowler said. "The information is helpful."

"That's not all Vincent had to say about Mrs. Elliott."

"What else?"

"Vincent waits tables at another restaurant in downtown Asheville, the Olde Town Inn, and he's seen Mrs. Elliott at that restaurant, as well. It was exactly a week earlier."

"Alone?"

"No, similar situation. She was with a man, both dressed for a night out."

"Same man?" Fowler asked.

"No, he was closer to her age, maybe late thirties or early forties, with long dark hair pulled into a man bun."

"Is he sure it was Sarah Elliott?"

"Vincent was waiting at an adjacent table, but he's positive. He said the dress she was wearing was revealing, and the couple was catching everyone's attention."

Fowler paused, digesting what he'd been told.

"You say this was exactly a week before he saw her at your restaurant?"

"Yes, a Thursday night, a week earlier."

"Tell Vincent thank you," he said. "With his observation skills, he has a future as a detective."

Fowler stood, phone in hand, staring across the kitchen.

These don't sound like dinner meetings. What was she up to? he wondered.

It was unclear if the new information about Sarah Elliott firmed up the case against her husband, or blurred it even more.

Fowler stepped to the refrigerator and lifted a bottle of beer from inside the door. He twisted off the cap and tossed it into the trash can in the corner of the room, using a bank shot off the wall. After taking a long draw on the bottle, he found an open bag of pretzels in a drawer, removed the clip, and went to his favorite recliner in the living room.

He wondered why Angela hadn't called.

Surely, she's home by now.

He took out his phone and hit her number.

"Your timing is perfect," she answered. "I just walked in the door."

"What did you learn from the FBI?"

"They suspect that MedEX is selling pain meds on the street and Cap INC is helping launder the funds."

"We sort of knew that already. Can they prove it?" Fowler asked.

"Not yet, but I get the feeling they're close."

"Did they have any idea what happened to Motts or to your informants?"

"Their guess is that Motts upset his superiors at Cap INC or an associate, but they have nothing to prove any of it," she replied. "How about you? What did you learn in Asheville?"

"I talked to an inmate, Desmond Leaks, who came to the same conclusion as your FBI agent. He said Motts didn't seem stressed and thinks he was given an overdose in his food. Leaks also doesn't believe Sarah Elliott's murder was a professional hit."

"It sounds like the popular opinion is Sarah was killed by someone she knows, and it was probably her husband," Jones said.

"Here's where the plot thickens," Fowler teased.

"What is it?"

"It looks like Rand wasn't the only Elliott finding companionship outside their marriage," Fowler replied. "I found a waiter who says he saw Sarah at the Vista View restaurant with an older dark-haired man, and then again at a downtown restaurant with a younger guy, both dressed for a night out on the town."

"You can't be serious."

"It gets better. Sarah checked into a room using a driver's license with the name Elle Dearing. She checked out the next morning, paying cash, accompanied by a man matching the description of her dinner guest from the night before."

"Have you checked the bill at the other restaurant to see if her name's on the receipt?" Jones asked.

"Not yet, but I will in the morning."

"Sounds like Sarah was double and triple-timing her husband. There may be more than one scorned lover who wanted revenge," Jones said.

"Possibly, but I've learned from watching *Dateline*, it's usually the husband," Fowler replied, failing to sound serious.

"Sad, but true," she chuckled. "So, where to from here?"

"In addition to checking out the downtown Asheville restaurant, I'm having surveillance video pulled at the Vista View Inn to see if Sarah and her companion show up."

"I guess I'll pay a call on the management at MedEX," Jones said. "I doubt they'll share much about Motts, but it's worth a shot."

"Any chance we can get together over the weekend?" Fowler asked.

"Maybe," she replied. "Let's see how tomorrow goes."

- DAY 8 -

Friday

THE DA, RON OLSEN, was inside Chief Pierce's office when Fowler arrived early Friday. From the slight opening in the door, he could see Olsen leaning, both hands on the chief's desk, yelling at Pierce, who was seated with his beefy arms crossed. With thinning, unruly hair and a beak-like nose, Olsen resembled a chicken hawk preying on an unyielding bear.

"I have no reason to doubt my sister-in-law!" Olsen yelled. "What the hell was Fowler doing at the Vista View Inn in Asheville? And right after our discussion with the mayor about staying within your jurisdiction."

Fowler paused, looking down the hall toward the detectives' bullpen, and then back inside Pierce's office. He briefly considered avoiding the confrontation taking place.

"Oh, what the hell," he said under his breath before stepping through the opening. "Can I be of some assistance, Chief?"

Olsen pulled back from the desk and wheeled around toward Fowler.

"It seems Mr. Olsen's sister-in-law over in Asheville is friends with Sharon Miller, the lady you met with yesterday at the Vista View Inn," Pierce calmly explained.

Fowler stepped further into the office and closed the door behind him as Pierce continued.

"She called Ron last night to see what he knew about the Elliott murder investigation. And while she was on the phone, she told our DA everything you apparently learned from her and her staff about Sarah Elliott. I assume you were going to update us this morning on what you uncovered."

"Are you suggesting I've done something wrong by discovering Sarah Elliott was seeing other men in the days before she was killed?"

"So, what my sister-in-law told me is true?" Olsen asked, throwing his hands skyward.

"If she told you that Vista View Inn employees have seen Sarah Elliott in the company of two different men at dinner, and apparently staying the night with one of them, then yes. She's told you what I uncovered. Some of what I learned was as late as eight o'clock last evening."

"I can't believe you'd be so careless that even my sister-in-law knew about this before I did," Olsen wailed.

"And how does this harm your case against Rand Elliott?" Fowler argued. "If anything, his wife's infidelity provides a motive for murder that you didn't have before."

Fowler's comeback caused Olsen to calm slightly.

"I hope you haven't run to Elliott's attorney with this information," Olsen warned.

"He's gonna learn about Sarah's trysts sooner or later," Fowler said. "But no, I don't intend to meet with Eldon Watkins anytime soon."

"Can I assume I've heard everything?" Olsen asked.

"I'm going to see what I can find out about Sarah's dinner at the Olde Town Inn," Fowler replied. "And I've also asked for surveillance video from the Vista View Inn during her checkout."

"Let me know immediately if you learn anything else," Olsen demanded.

"You'll know immediately after I inform Chief Pierce," Fowler replied.

Olsen glanced at Pierce, then back to Fowler.

"No more surprises," he said, stomping from the office.

"I would have called you last night," Fowler said. "But it was getting late, and I knew you had a lot on your plate with Jenkins being in the hospital."

"I'm not concerned with Olsen," Pierce said. "He suffers from a Napolean complex and is struggling to live up to the expectations of his congressman father."

"How's Jenkins doing?" Fowler asked.

"Not well, I'm afraid. I was only able to look in on him for a minute yesterday afternoon. He knew I was there, but we couldn't talk."

"What about Abby? How's she holding up?"

"She's being strong in front of her husband, but she broke down several times in the waiting room," Pierce replied. "She called her son in Colorado, asking him to come. He'll be here tonight."

"Jenkins is a tough guy. He'll pull through, won't he?" Fowler asked.

"I sure hope so."

- 8.1-

DETECTIVE JONES was unable to find a phone number on MedEX's website where a real person would answer, so she elected to drive to the address listed as its manufacturing headquarters.

Her car's GPS led her to the far east side of Charlotte and into the center of an expansive warehouse district. Dozens and dozens of metal buildings, each the size of a football field, were clustered in an area just outside the city's outer loop. It wasn't the kind of place you'd expect to find a high-tech pharmaceutical company.

Street addresses around the warehouses were poorly marked, and her GPS had become useless. She drove up and down roads between sprawling buildings until coming to a structure with a redbrick front and a low sign near the road that read: *MedEX Pharmaceuticals.* Jones pulled her Volvo into the parking lot and found an empty spot near the double glass doors at the front of the building.

The doors were locked, and a badge reader was positioned near the entrance. Jones looked for a phone or a button to solicit help, but found none. She cupped her hands around her face, pressed her nose to the glass, and peered into the building.

The lobby was sparsely furnished with a blue faux leather sofa and midcentury modern chrome chairs on either side. There was no receptionist or anyone else in the lobby.

She waited at the entrance until a young black woman with dark, straight hair pulled into a ponytail approached. She was dressed in a white blouse, denim jacket, and jeans. Reaching the entrance, she slid the badge hanging from a lanyard around her neck into the card reader and the door snapped open.

Jones flashed her SBI badge toward the young woman.

"Miss, I'm Detective Angela Jones with the SBI, and I need to speak with the manager of this facility."

The woman reached out, took the badge from Jones, and studied it. As the sleeve of her jacket slid back, Jones noticed a small tattoo of a yellow rose on her right wrist.

"I'm sorry, but I'm not authorized to let anyone inside," she said, returning the badge. "I'll see if I can find someone to help you."

Without waiting for a response, the woman quickly disappeared into the building and the door swung shut behind her.

Jones paced up and down the sidewalk, reading emails on her phone, waiting for someone to appear. Ten minutes elapsed before a tall middle-aged gentleman in a sport coat and wrinkled khaki slacks stepped outside. He had thinning hair and wore thick, dark-rimmed glasses that he repeatedly pressed to his face with his index finger.

"I'm Jeremy Wilson. I understand you're looking to speak to someone. May I ask what this is regarding?"

"I'm Detective Angela Jones, and I'm investigating the death of Malone Motts, who I believe was the manager of this facility," Jones replied.

"Yes. He was in charge of operations at this site," Wilson replied. "Mr. Statler is our CEO."

"What's your role at MedEX?"

"I worked for Mr. Motts. I oversee distribution."

"Would it be possible for me to meet with Mr. Statler today?" Jones asked.

"His office is in another building. Is there anything I can help you with?" Wilson replied. "There's a conference room just off the lobby where we could talk."

"I do have several questions if you don't mind."

"Come this way," he said, leading Jones inside and through the lobby into a drab, windowless room with a table and six chairs. The room's walls were off-white and smudged. The floor was covered in 12-inch-square linoleum tile with a multi-colored amoeba pattern from the 1950s. A photo taken from a drone high above the facility hung on the wall as the only décor item.

"We were shocked to learn of Mr. Motts' death," Wilson began.

"What about his arrest?" Jones asked. "Would you have expected your manager to be in possession of five kilos of fentanyl?"

"Of course not," he replied. "Mr. Motts had been with MedEX several years and was well respected."

"Can you come up with any explanation as to how the drugs ended up in Motts' car?"

"Illegal drugs are becoming more and more plentiful. I imagine Mr. Motts had contacts on the street," Wilson said. "I guess he was looking to make a quick score."

"You just said you'd never expect Motts to be in possession of illegal drugs."

"Five kilos of fentanyl go for five million on the street. If a dealer gets ten percent, that's half a mil," he replied. "Money can make anyone do crazy things."

"Is that the general belief around here?" Jones asked. "That Motts decided to risk his job and make a quick buck?"

"Yeah. I guess. What other explanation could there be?"

"What if it was planted in his car by someone out to get him—to put him in prison for a long time?"

"That's ridiculous," he scoffed. "Who'd have the kinda money to spend five million to frame someone?"

"Someone very powerful," Jones replied. "Someone who wanted Motts out of the way because he represented an even larger risk. Would you know anyone like that?"

Wilson's head snapped back, appearing stunned by Jones' boldness.

"Do I look like the kinda guy who knows people willing to throw away five million bucks?" Wilson asked, pushing his glasses back to his face.

"What about people who were at odds with your former boss? Were you aware of anyone who saw him as a threat or had disagreements with him?"

"No. Not a soul," Wilson quickly replied.

"One final question," she said. "Who took Malone Motts' position at MedEX?"

"I'm in that role now," he said. "Why?"

"Just curious."

"I've already been gone too long," Wilson said, rattled by Jones' last statement. "Can you find your own way back out?"

"Certainly."

They stepped out of the room with Wilson turning left and Jones turning right toward the sparsely furnished lobby. As she was about to push open the glass door to the outside, she felt a tap on her shoulder. She pivoted to see the young lady she'd met out front earlier.

"I can't talk here," she said. "Take this and call me at home tonight."

The young woman pressed a piece of paper into Jones' hand, then turned and disappeared down a long hallway.

Jones waited until she reached her car to look at what she'd been given. All that was written on the paper was a phone number and note that read:

Something big is going down soon. People may die.

- 8.2 -

FAILING TO GET ANYTHING done over the phone, Detective Fowler drove his sedan back toward Asheville. He'd been told by a member of the cleaning staff who answered his call that James Beckley, the manager of the Olde Town Inn and Restaurant, came in shortly before eleven when it opened for lunch.

An irregular beat from the sedan's balding tires beating against the pavement filled the cabin of the car. Even with the distraction of the traffic and the colorful fall scenery, Fowler couldn't get the thought of his partner clinging to life out of his mind.

Sixty had once seemed ancient to the young detective, but not any longer. And to him, Jenkins was a young 60, surely too young to be taken by pneumonia. He would make a point to stop by Stonefield General when he got back to town.

FOWLER MERGED off I-40 and wound his way toward downtown.

Asheville had done a masterful job of preserving its history and architecture. The narrow streets of the arts and restaurant districts were lined with century-old brick buildings that had been brought back to life, allowing visitors to feel as if they were stepping back into the past. Such was the street occupied by the Olde Town Inn and Restaurant.

There was no parking near the entrance of the four-story inn, requiring Fowler to find a nearby municipal lot. Tourists milled about the streets as he walked back toward the hotel. Several out-of-towners read the menus posted outside restaurants lining the street.

The lobby of the 40-room hotel was cozy and tastefully decorated with period furnishings from the 1800s, but it lacked the spacious opulence of the Vista View Inn. Fowler stepped around guests and gawkers to get to the information counter staffed by a wiry, white-haired gentleman in a white shirt and red vest.

"I'm Detective Jack Fowler, and I'm looking for James Beckley," he said, discretely flashing his badge.

The man behind the counter smiled.

"Well, you've found him. And you can call me Jim," the diminutive man said. "I hope I'm not in any trouble."

"You're the manager?"

"It's stranger than that," he replied. "I own this hotel. We're a little short on help these days, so I figured there was no one better to staff the information counter than me. How can I help you?"

"I'm looking for information on a gentleman who dined with this woman at your restaurant a few weeks ago. Her name is Sarah Elliott," he said softly, handing the photo to him. "I've written the time and date they were here on the back."

"I can't say that I recognize her," he replied.

"Vincent, one of your waiters, confirmed they were here."

"May I ask why you need information about the man this woman was with?"

Fowler scanned the area, making sure no one was eavesdropping.

"Ms. Elliott was murdered a week ago and this man may be able to provide information related to the investigation," Fowler replied.

"Is he a suspect?"

"Not at this time. We have a suspect under arrest, and I'm just tying up loose ends on the case."

"What can I do?"

"I'm hoping the gentleman paid for the dinner that night with a credit card," Fowler replied. "If he did, I'd like to see if you could find the transaction in your billing system."

"You're looking for his name?"

"And his home address listed on the credit card if it's available."

"This is highly unusual and not something we typically provide," Beckley replied.

"I could ask my police chief to give you a call if you have any doubts."

The white-haired owner studied Fowler for a brief moment.

"Can I see that badge one more time?" he asked.

Fowler placed the gold shield on the counter facing him.

"I'll have someone look for the information. Here's a coupon for a free lunch. Have a seat over there," he said, pointing to indoor café tables near the front window. "I'll make sure a waiter gets to you quickly."

FOWLER FELT a little guilty enjoying one of the best Reuben sandwiches he'd ever tasted as he waited for someone to provide the information he requested. Watching others around him dining on crab cakes and drinking Chardonnay on a workday, he wondered what they did when they weren't kicking back in Asheville.

Maybe this is all they do, he thought.

As he dipped his last fried potato slice into a pool of ketchup, a young woman in a red vest with her auburn hair pulled back approached.

"Detective Fowler?" she asked, as he wiped ketchup from his chin.

"Yes."

"I think I've found what you're looking for," she said, handing him a computer printout. "Here's the gentleman's name and address. I was also able to find a phone number."

Fowler read the information.

"This is perfect. I really appreciate your help."

"No problem, sir. My pleasure," she said, turning and walking toward the front counter.

He finished his tea, left a $10 tip, and hurried toward the entrance. A line had formed in front of James Beckley at the information desk, so Fowler waved and mouthed "thank you" to the gracious hotel owner.

The man's name on the printout was Richard Ashley and his address was in Charlotte. As soon as Fowler reached the privacy of his car, he punched in the phone number.

"This is Richard," a man answered on the third ring.

"Mr. Ashley, I'm Detective Jack Fowler with Stonefield PD."

"You're a detective?"

"That's right."

"Am I in some kind of trouble?"

"No, sir. I'm just looking for information about Sarah Elliott."

"I don't know anyone by that name."

Fowler thought for a minute.

"What about Elle Dearing? Is that name familiar?"

Silence.

"Mr. Ashley, are you still there?"

"Yeah, I'm here. What do you want to know?" he asked, his tone becoming defensive.

"Can you confirm you dined with her at the Olde Town Inn about three weeks ago?"

"Yeah, we had dinner, but that's as far as it went."

"How is it you know Ms. Dearing?"

"Listen! I told you all I did was have dinner with her," he replied irritably.

"Can you at least confirm how you met?"

"She advertises on DearingDates.com, but no laws were broken," he replied. "We had dinner and I drove back to Charlotte. She was gorgeous, but her price was too steep for me."

Damn! She was a hooker!

The conversation finally made sense to Fowler.

"Did you have any contact with Ms. Dearing either before or after the dinner at the Olde Town Inn?"

"We exchanged a couple of texts to set up our meeting, but that was it."

"You've provided all I need to know for now. I'll get back to you if there's anything else," Fowler said.

"That's it?"

"Yeah. For now."

Fowler brought up the web browser on his cellphone and typed in *DearingDates.com.*

There was no question about what services were being offered. A picture of Sarah Elliott was not included. Instead, an electronic form was provided for interested gentlemen to complete and return. Photos of Ms. Dearing would be forwarded once a background check was completed.

Before Fowler could put the phone back into his jacket, he received a call.

"Detective, this is Sharon Miller."

"I was just heading your direction."

"I think I can save you the trip. We found the video of when Sarah Elliott was checking out."

"That's great. Can you see the gentleman she was with?" he asked.

"Yes. He's in frame, but his face is not revealed—only side and back views."

"I'd still like to see it."

"Our IT guy was able to copy it into a video clip, and he forwarded it to your email," she replied. "He said you should be able to bring it up easily. If not, his number is in the email."

"Thanks, this will save me some time today."

FOWLER COULDN'T wait until he returned to Stonefield PD to tell Chief Pierce what he'd uncovered. He hit Pierce's number.

"Hello, Jack. I was about to give you a call."

The chief's somber tone sent Fowler's heart to his throat.

"What is it?"

"I just heard from Abby Jenkins. Brooks died from an apparent heart attack about an hour ago."

Fowler sank back into the car seat, staring out the windshield, his stomach knotting.

"I'm stunned."

It was all he could say.

"We all are, Jack. My heart aches for Abby, but when I spoke with her, she was more concerned for her son. He didn't get here in time. He's in the air and will learn of his father's death when he lands in Greensboro."

For a brief moment, Fowler froze. The confusion and hopelessness Fowler felt was similar to past PTSD episodes, but the anxiety and visions that paralyzed him then weren't there. It took a few seconds to gather his thoughts.

"I'd be glad to pick him up, but I'm three hours from Greensboro," Fowler said.

"Abby wants to tell her son in person. I'm going to drive her to the airport in a few minutes.

"You called me," Pierce continued. "What did you want to tell me?"

"You sure you want to hear now?" Fowler asked.

"As long as you can tell me in less than five minutes."

"I think I've discovered something that may impact the Elliott case. It appears Sarah Elliott was not only seeing other men, she was charging for her services."

"Just when I thought I couldn't be surprised, you managed to prove me wrong," Pierce said. "You're sure about this?"

"I'm positive. I've seen her posts on DearingDates.com and talked to one of her clients. It appears she was leading two lives, one at home and a parallel life outside of Stonefield."

155

"This might open up the field to other suspects," Pierce said. "She wouldn't be the first prostitute to lose her life to one of her johns."

"True."

"I need to go, but make sure you inform Olsen," Pierce said.

"I will, as soon as I get back to town."

- 8.3 -

THE MOOD AT SPD headquarters was solemn when Fowler returned. Everyone moved about the office in slow motion, sadness and disbelief etched on their faces. A twenty-five-year veteran of the force and a friend to all was gone. It had only been a few hours since Jenkins' passing, but flowers and cards were already gathering at his cubicle. Fowler paused to observe the makeshift memorial. He felt his emotions rushing to the surface, forcing him to take a deep breath and step away.

He decided to wait before calling Jones, not wanting to disrupt her workday. Jenkins and Jones had only met a couple of times, but they had a bond and a respect for each other. They shared similar experiences as groundbreakers in their field.

He sat at his cubicle for several minutes, working up the motivation to get back to work.

Before contacting the DA, Fowler decided to look at the video clip sent to him by the IT guy from the Vista View Inn. He logged into his email and found the note near the top of the queue. When he clicked on the icon, the video began instantly.

The full-screen image lacked audio and showed Sarah Elliott dressed in a dark pantsuit with a travel bag over her shoulder, standing at the checkout counter. The surveillance camera was focused on the people at and around the counter.

About fifteen feet behind Sarah stood a man wearing an open collar shirt and dark sport coat with grey slacks. Other than the man's dark hair and average build, it was impossible to detect detailed features.

Fowler continued to watch as the man waited impatiently for Sarah to complete her transaction. He shifted his weight from side to side and fidgeted with his collar and shirt cuffs, but at no time did he turn and face her. It was as if he was aware of the camera.

Sarah turned and approached the gentleman. They exchanged a few words and then walked together out of camera range toward the hotel entrance.

The video was further confirmation of Sarah's rendezvous, but provided little new information. Fowler forwarded the video clip to SBI Forensics in Greensboro to see if they could enlarge and enhance the images.

Fowler pulled out his cellphone and hit Ron Olsen's number.

"Hello, Jack. Sorry to hear about Jenkins."

"Yeah. Everyone's in shock right now," Fowler replied. "He'll be missed. It'll be a while before things get back to normal around here."

"I can imagine."

"Say, I just got back from Asheville and have some news about Sarah Elliott."

"What's that?"

"I've confirmed that she wasn't just dating other men. She was selling her services as a personal escort."

"Shit! Are you saying she was a hooker?"

"Exactly. I talked with one of her clients and found her ad on her website, DearingDates.com. There's no doubt about what she was doing," Fowler replied. "I'll send you the link. Her working girl name was Elle Dearing."

"This adds an illegal and seedy element to the case, but I'm not sure it alters the charges against Rand Elliott," Olsen said. "If anything, it provides motivation as to why Rand killed his wife."

"It will also allow the defense to argue that a disgruntled john could've taken revenge against Sarah," Fowler argued.

"The defense would need to provide evidence that this disgruntled person existed."

"True, but you have to admit it clouds the case and removes an element of sympathy for the victim," Fowler said.

"That's why we need to keep this under wraps for now. The last thing I need is for this salacious story to hit the press. They'd have a field day with it."

"I've only told you and the chief," Fowler replied. "But the story is out there for anyone enterprising enough to find it."

"Let's hope they don't."

- 8.4 -

IT WAS LATE AFTERNOON and Detective Jones was back at her office, chomping at the bit to talk to the woman with the rose on her wrist she'd met at MedEX. Jones had tried calling her earlier, but received a generic voicemail in a male voice, saying, *"The party you called is not available. To receive a call back, leave a message and your number."* Jones did neither.

She assumed the female employee was still at work and unable to answer. The woman didn't provide her name, only a phone number and cryptic message about something going down and lives being in danger.

While Jones waited, she tried to connect the phone number to a name or address by going to her computer and doing a white pages reverse search. This program had worked for her in the past to locate people using only their phone numbers.

She entered the number from the slip of paper on the search line and hit enter.

> *No information is available for this number. It could be unlisted or the associated cellphone is not registered with a carrier.*

Not registered was another way of saying the phone was intended for temporary use. It was likely a burner phone, often used to hide the identity of the owner.

Jones waited until 5:00 p.m. and called the number one more time. Again, she received a generic greeting. This time she left her name and cellphone number before packing up her desk and heading home.

JONES PULLED INTO the garage and shut the door behind her. She didn't like jogging in the dark, but she needed to work off her frustrations. She changed into running clothes with reflective strips and slipped on her New Balance shoes. With her cellphone clipped to her belt, she headed out the front door.

Her neighborhood wasn't gated, but access was limited to only two entrances at opposite ends of the housing development. She felt safe as long as she remained on local streets and sidewalks.

It was a calm, cool night. Ten minutes into her run, she heard a car approaching from behind. The dark grey BMW with tinted windows slowed to a crawl and followed alongside of her for half a block. She turned to look, but was unable to see anyone through the dark windows.

The longer the sedan followed her, the more frightened she became. She felt her heart rate increase as she looked for escape routes.

Jones normally ran with a canister of Mace clipped at her waist, but in her haste, she'd overlooked bringing it. She stopped under the streetlights at the next corner. The car paused with her. Her heart pounded, both from the run and the threat of her unknown stalker. She thought about bolting to the nearest house, but instead, took her cellphone from the clip on her belt and dialed 911. As the dispatcher came on the line, the car sped ahead toward the neighborhood exit.

"This is nine-one-one. What's your emergency?"

She thought for a moment, and then replied, "There is no emergency. My mistake."

In the darkness, Jones was unable to get a clear view of the tag as the car sped off. She made a mental note that the vehicle following her was a dark grey BMW 730i.

Angela reversed course and ran back home. With her adrenalin surging, the return run took her a minute less.

Her hands quivered as she entered the security passcode and opened the front door. She went straight to the kitchen and removed her gun holster from the wall peg and slipped it on. After pouring a glass of Chardonnay, Angela returned to the living room, sat in her favorite chair, and took several sips.

A couple of minutes later, her heart rate had calmed. She set the wineglass on a side table and called Jack.

"I was getting concerned that you hadn't called," Jack said.

"It's been quite a day," she replied. "And it just got more exciting."

"What's going on?"

"I went to MedEX this morning. It took a while, but I finally talked with Jeremy Wilson who took Malone Motts' job."

"Was he open to a discussion?"

"Yeah. He was willing to talk, but the general consensus at MedEX is Motts was trying to make a quick score selling drugs and got caught."

"What about his death?"

"It seemed clear Wilson agreed with the suicide report," she replied. "I suggested that Motts was being framed, but he disagreed."

"Was that it?"

"No. I thought I'd found a whistleblower," she replied. "When I was leaving, a woman came up from behind and pressed a note into my hand. I have it right here. It has her phone number and a note that says: *Something big is going down soon. People may die*."

"Have you called her?"

"I haven't been able to reach her," she replied. "I tried to get an address or a name by doing a reverse search on the phone number, but no luck."

"Maybe she'll call back later."

"I hope so," she replied. "But that's not all. I just went for a quick run and a dark BMW stalked me for a block or so, and then it paused beside me when I stopped at the corner."

"Did you get a tag number?"

"No. It was too dark."

"Do you think this has anything to do with your visit to MedEX?"

"I don't know what to think," she replied. "But I have a bad feeling about that company. From the time I pulled into the parking lot, I felt something was wrong."

"I think this would be a good weekend to hang out together," he said. "I also have some news to share."

"What's that?"

"Brooks Jenkins died from a heart attack this morning."

"Oh my God! Everyone must be in shock."

"To say the least. Pierce drove Jenkins' wife to the airport to pick up her son this afternoon. He didn't get back in time to see his father before he died."

The thought of a son losing his father caused Jones to pause. She wiped a tear from her eye and took a deep breath.

"What can we do?" she asked.

"I imagine Abby will need time alone with her son, but maybe by Sunday we can stop by," Jack said. "I'll check with Chief Pierce tomorrow and see what he thinks."

"Okay," she replied, holding back tears. "I'll pack a few things and be there in a couple hours."

"I'd be glad to drive your way," Jack said.

"No. I'm still a little creeped out by the stalker. I'd relax better at your place."

- 8.5 -

"I SAW ONE OF OUR employees, Rose Ratcliff, with a female detective who met with me today. I have her on surveillance video handing the cop something."

Jeremy Wilson had just called Jerald Jefferson, the executive at Cap INC in charge of cleaning up the Malone Motts mess. Jefferson sat in his opulent corner office in south Charlotte, poring over financial reports, his suitcoat off and his tie loosened.

"What female cop?" Jefferson asked, pulling off his tie. "What are you talking about?"

"Her name is Jones, Detective Angela Jones. She came looking for you. Actually, she was looking for Mr. Statler."

"Be careful what you're saying on an open line," Jefferson warned. "What specifically did this cop want?"

"She was asking questions about Motts. She wanted to know what I thought about his arrest, and if I believed he was set up."

"And what did you say?"

"I said of course not," Wilson replied, nervously adjusting his glasses. "I told her that Motts must've gotten greedy."

"Did she buy it?"

"I think so, but I'm not sure."

"You better be damn sure no one finds out about you planting the fentanyl," Jefferson growled.

"No one knows," Wilson replied. "I'm sure."

"Motts had to be replaced because he was having trouble following my directions and was pushing back on the new formula," Jefferson said. "If you get careless, you can also be replaced."

Wilson nervously fidgeted with a pen as perspiration beaded on his balding head.

"I'm also concerned about the pain med changes," he said. "It's nearly ready to ship, but with all this attention from the cops, are you sure we want to proceed?"

"The boss says ship it!" Jefferson shouted. "We've already set up Motts as the fall guy. It's his name on the authorization forms. If adverse effects are experienced, we'll just point to your former boss."

"Adverse effects? More like death," Wilson mumbled louder than he'd intended.

"What was that?" Jefferson snapped.

"Nothing," he replied, pulling a handkerchief from his pocket and patting his head.

"Tell me about this employee who spoke with the detective," Jefferson said.

"Her name is Rose Ratcliff. She's an entry-level lab technician," Wilson replied. "I checked the surveillance video from the lobby to make sure Jones left promptly, and I saw her give the cop something."

"Where's Ratcliff now?"

"She's in a conference room next to my office. I told her she was being investigated for a security breach," Wilson replied. "And she was not to call or speak to anyone until I got back to her."

"Did you ask what she gave the detective?"

"She claimed it was something Jones had dropped, and she was just returning it."

"Do you believe her?"

"I'd like to, but she seems to be hiding something. There's also earlier video of Jones speaking with Ratcliff in front of the building."

Seconds of silence.

Jefferson gritted his teeth and stared across his office with a dark-eyed look of resolve. The words of Erik Rolland echoed inside his head—*Make sure the Motts mess is cleaned up!*

"Hold her in the room," he told Wilson. "I'll have someone pick her up within the hour."

- 8.6 -

REPEATED CALLS FROM JONES to the number on the slip of paper failed to reach anyone. The ponytailed MedEX employee with a tattooed rose on her wrist was not answering. Jones made her final attempt right before retiring for the evening.

Fowler and Jones lay in bed, neither able to fall asleep. Jack was on his back, staring at the ceiling fan. Jones was beside him, her head on his shoulder, with one arm draped over his chest.

"I can't slow my mind down," Jones said softly. "I keep thinking about how Jenkins' wife and son must be feeling. I've lost my parents, but they were older, and I saw it coming."

"The death of someone close to you is never easy," Fowler replied. "It's little comfort, but Jenkins and his wife spent more than thirty years together. Think of all the cops killed on the job in their prime. They leave home in the morning, and don't come back that night."

"Do you think about that, Jack?"

"Not coming home at night? Sure. I'd be lying if I said I didn't. But I worry about you more."

Jones raised her head and stared at Fowler.

"Don't," she said. "How can we be together if we live our lives in constant worry?"

"So, you don't worry about me?"

"Sometimes, but the thought of something happening to you doesn't affect how I live my life. I have confidence in you."

"And I in you," he said. "But worrying is in my DNA. I'll try not to let it show."

Jones lowered her head back to his shoulder. They lay in silence for a long moment, with only the rumble of traffic in the distance.

"It's looking like your murder case is close to wrapping up," she said. "While the Motts case continues to gain steam."

"At this point, I'd agree," he said. "There's a strong case against Rand Elliott. Unless one of Sarah's clients pops out of the woodwork, Rand's on his way to federal prison."

"It seems like every time I go to interview someone about Motts, they end up dead or they disappear," she said. "I hope the gal with the rose on her wrist is okay."

"You think she's in danger?"

"She seemed very nervous, almost panicky," Jones replied. "After giving me that slip of paper, she turned and ran off like a deer fleeing a wolf."

"Tomorrow is a weekend, but I assume a pharmaceutical manufacturer would operate seven days a week."

"What are you thinking?" Jones asked, raising her head again.

"I'm thinking if you don't hear from the rose lady, we should go see if someone at MedEX can tell us where she lives."

"What about paying a visit on Jenkins' wife and son?"

"I'll call Pierce in the morning and see how they're doing," Fowler replied.

"I say we take them something fresh from the bakery in the morning, and if they want company, we stay for a while."

169

"What about the rose lady?" Fowler asked.

"We can still drive to MedEX in the afternoon," she replied. "It's less than ninety minutes away."

"Okay. We've got a plan," Fowler said, kissing her forehead. "Let's get to sleep."

- DAY 9 -

Saturday

FOWLER WAS THE first to rise. Jones found him in the den seated in front of a desktop PC, fully dressed, with a cup of coffee in his hand.

"What time is it, anyway?" she asked, stretching at the doorway.

Fowler squinted at the clock on the computer.

"Quarter after seven," he said.

She approached, her hair in tangles, wearing Fowler's t-shirt, and gave him a peck on the neck.

"Give me that coffee," she said. "What are you doing, anyway?"

"I woke around five and couldn't doze back off," he replied. "I thought I'd try searching for anything on MedEX and its executive team."

"Find anything?" she asked, taking a sip.

"Not much. There's a lot out there about its products, and they boast about their technology being state-of-the-art, but I can't find a damn thing about the CEO, James Statler, or anyone who reports to him for that matter."

"That's strange," she said. "Hell, you Google me and you get three screens of stuff."

A new email notice popped on the screen, catching Fowler's attention. It was from the forensic team leader in Greensboro.

"It looks like the tech guys were able to enhance the video clip from the Vista View Inn," Fowler said. "Let me see if it'll display on my computer."

Fowler clicked on the video icon as Jones stepped closer and watched over his right shoulder.

"It's working!"

The video of the man behind Sarah Elliott was much clearer than before and at least 30% larger.

"Is that the guy she was with?" she asked.

"Yeah. That's him in the dark jacket. I wish he'd turn toward the camera," Fowler replied. "So far, his face isn't visible enough to ID him, or to get a still photo to distribute."

"He keeps messing with his shirtsleeves and adjusting his collar," Jones said. "His nervous tics would drive me nuts."

The video ended with Sarah Elliott walking toward the entrance with the dark-haired man at her side.

"The enhancements didn't help much," Fowler said. "But I still feel like I've met this guy before. There's something about his tics, or maybe it's his gait. He's in constant motion."

"I'm gonna hop in the shower," Jones said, placing the coffee cup onto the desk. "When's breakfast served?"

Fowler grinned.

"I'll see what I can put together," he replied. "Are scrambled eggs okay?"

"Perfect. I'll be there in twenty."

Fowler sat, thinking. He pulled up the video one more time and watched it closely. Nothing was clicking with him, so he powered down the PC and headed to the kitchen.

JONES APPEARED dressed for the day as Fowler set breakfast on the table.

"Dig in before it gets cold," he said.

"I just tried calling the number again," Jones said, taking a seat. "The message has changed. It now says this number is no longer in service."

"You know there's a chance the woman has just changed her mind about talking with you. Whistleblowers can be unpredictable."

"I think it's more likely someone changed her mind *for* her," Jones argued.

"Maybe we should get a search warrant."

"Do you think we could? All we have is a tip from an unknown woman saying something is going down."

"Yeah, you're probably right," Fowler replied. "Although the note did say people may die."

"I don't want to wait for a warrant. Surely we can find someone who knows the woman without needing a warrant."

Fowler's cellphone chirped on the kitchen counter. The caller ID was Chief Pierce.

"Good morning, Chief. How are Abby and her son doing? We were thinking about taking something over to eat later this morning."

Jones focused on Fowler's face, trying to follow the conversation.

"That's why I called," Pierce said. "Abby is having a tough time, and her doctor has given her something to help her relax. Her son, Kerry, asked me to let people know that she needs to rest for a day or two."

"Sorry to hear she's not doing well, but it's understandable."

"Funeral plans are still up in the air, but services won't be until Tuesday or later," Pierce added. "I'll need to arrange schedules to allow as many from the force to attend as possible."

"I'm sure the turnout will be large," Fowler said, "if the flowers and cards at his desk are any indication."

"This weekend might be a good time for everyone to take a short break from work," Pierce said. "Jenkins' death has put a whole new perspective on things."

There was silence as Fowler looked to Jones. Neither wanted to take a break from their investigations.

"I think Jenkins would want us to move forward," Fowler said. "He knew how important our work was."

"True. He did."

"Thanks for calling," Fowler said.

"Something wrong with Abby?" Jones asked.

"Pierce said she needs a day or two of rest."

"Why didn't you tell him about us planning a visit to MedEX today?"

"He asked that I not focus on the Motts case, and I didn't want to upset him. Besides, I'm just your driver."

IT WAS A SUNNY day, lifting the spirits of Jones and Fowler as they drove south to Charlotte. Fall had refused to yield to colder temperatures, and it felt more like May than the first week of October.

Jones was able to direct Fowler through the maze of buildings to the front of MedEX Pharmaceuticals. The parking lot had half as many cars as yesterday, but it appeared the site was operational. At that moment, no one was entering or leaving through the double doors of the sprawling one-story metal building. They would have to wait for someone to let them in.

After several minutes, Jones and Fowler stepped from his vehicle and walked to the entrance. Fowler pressed his face to the glass door and scanned the empty lobby.

"This dump looks nothing like the website," Fowler said. "It's hard to believe anything high-tech is developed inside there."

He searched the card reader for a visitor's button to push, but found nothing. Looking up, he could see two surveillance cameras high on the wall of the building.

"Someone knows we're out here," he said. "Let's hold our badges to the camera to see if that gets a response."

Looking serious, they extended their shields to the camera on the right.

"There must be fifty cars in that lot," Jones said. "I can't believe there's not one person coming or going."

Ten minutes later, the front door swung open and a large man with muscled forearms appeared. He was dressed in dark slacks and a short-sleeved white dress shirt with ARCO security patches on the shoulder. A tin badge was stuck to his chest. Fowler stood over six feet tall and weighed 180 pounds, but the guard dwarfed him.

"I saw your badges in the camera," he said. "What do you want?"

Jones stepped forward.

"This is Detective Fowler and I'm Detective Jones with the SBI," she began. "I was here yesterday and met with a Mr. Wilson regarding the arrest and death of Malone Motts."

"I knew Mr. Motts," he replied in a gravelly voice. "Too bad what happened to him. So, why are you back today?"

"I was given this note on my way out yesterday by a young woman. She didn't identify herself, but she appeared desperate. I've tried repeatedly to reach her at the number on the paper, but no one answers. I was hoping someone at MedEX could provide her name or her address."

"Do you have an appointment with anyone?" he asked.

"No, but could you try to contact Mr. Wilson, the site manager I met with yesterday?"

"He's not here today."

"There must be a manager on duty at a site this large," Jones said. "Could you let that person know we're here?"

The guard looked down at the note Jones had given him.

"I guess I could let Mr. Stevens know you're out here," he said. "He works for Mr. Wilson."

"If you have his number, I could call him," Jones offered.

"I don't think he'd want me giving out his company number," he replied, handing the note back to Jones. "Wait here. I'll see what I can do."

"I'm betting Mr. Stevens never shows," Fowler said.

After several more minutes passed, a young man in his twenties wearing a blue dress shirt and slacks walked out the door.

"Mr. Stevens?" Jones asked.

"No," the young man replied, looking startled. "Are you expecting him?"

"We'd spoken to a security guard who was going to let Mr. Stevens know we were here."

"Well, good luck," the man said as he began to step away.

"Wait," Jones called. "Maybe you can help us."

He stopped and turned back.

"What is it you're looking for?"

"It's not what. It's who," Jones said, extending her badge. "We're detectives investigating the death of Malone Motts."

The young man's head snapped back, appearing stunned.

"I heard he committed suicide. Was he murdered?"

"Like I said, we're investigating his death," Jones replied.

"I'm in a hurry, but I'll try to help if I can."

Jones provided the young man the same information she'd given the security guard and handed him the note.

"What did she look like?" he asked.

"Attractive black woman, early thirties, straight hair in a ponytail, and she had a yellow rose tattooed under her wrist."

His face fell, as if being told his dog had died.

"Her name's Rose Ratcliff," he said. "I used to work with her."

"That's her real name?"

"Yes."

"Can you tell us anything else about her? Her address?" Jones asked.

"Don't know where she lives, but there's one thing you should know."

"What's that?"

"She was dating Malone Motts."

JONES AND FOWLER didn't wait for Mr. Stevens or the security guard to return. They hurried back to the car, and Jones began searching for Rose Ratcliff's address on her cellphone.

"I think I've found it," Jones said. "Twenty-one Blackstone Lane. It's only a few miles from here."

With the Australian male voice on Google Maps announcing the route, Fowler sped through the streets of east Charlotte. They reached their destination in less than 15 minutes.

Blackstone Lane was a narrow street in a blue-collar neighborhood, the kind you'd expect to find on a TV sitcom like *Everybody Loves Raymond*. The trees were large and the yards were small. The homes were well-maintained, but modest.

A late-model blue Toyota was parked under the carport beside a small, one-story, white bungalow. The number 21 was posted beside the front door.

Fowler pulled to the curb and stopped.

"Looks like she's home," he said.

They both stepped from the car and approached the front door. He knocked firmly three times, but no one answered. There was silence on the other side of the door.

"Rose Ratcliff, this is Detective Jones with the SBI. Come out now!"

Still no answer.

Fowler tried the door, but it was locked. He reached into the pocket of his jacket and pulled out a small box. Inside were miniature tools resembling bent metal toothpicks.

"What are you doing?" Jones asked.

"What does it look like? I'm going to open this door."

Fowler knelt and inserted one of the picks into the lock. After a few pokes and turns, the doorknob turned and the door swung open.

Standing in the entry, they could see a woman, facedown on the living room sofa. Rose Ratcliff was wearing the same jeans and denim jacket as the day before.

Jones moved quickly to the woman's side and placed two fingers to her neck. She looked at Fowler and shook her head.

"She's dead," Jones said.

On a coffee table in front of the sofa was an open prescription bottle of drugs. Several pills were spilled onto the table. Fowler started to reach for the bottle.

"Wait!" Jones warned. "Do you have gloves?"

"In the car. I'll be right back."

He returned and handed a pair of blue latex gloves to Jones and pulled a pair onto his hands. Being careful to remember the original position of the bottle, he picked it up and read the label.

"MedEX opioids," he said. "No prescription or date."

Jones found a white notecard on the floor beside the sofa. She knelt to pick it up.

"Now we're back together," Jones read.

"That's all it says?"

Jones handed the note to Fowler.

"Looks like a woman's writing," he said, handing the note back.

Jones took out the scrap of paper she'd been given by Ratcliff yesterday.

"The handwriting matches," she said.

They both stood in place and silently scanned the home. The house was neat, clean, and well-furnished. Everything seemed to be in place.

"I'm not buying this," Jones said. "The woman I saw yesterday was scared, not depressed."

"This is your case. You'd better phone it in," Fowler said.

JONES AND FOWLER waited out front on the steps as Charlotte-Mecklenburg PD squad cars sped up the street, lights flashing, sirens off.

"What do we have here?" the larger of the two uniformed officers asked.

Jones flashed her SBI badge and recited the history of the case to the officer. Fowler admitted to picking the lock, but said they had reason to believe Ratcliff's life was in jeopardy. The officers searched the home and yard, but found no evidence of a break-in.

Hours later, the CSI team completed processing the home. There wasn't much to find.

As neighbors gawked from across the street, the coroner loaded Ratcliff's body into a white van. Jones stepped to the van and talked with the coroner and the lead forensic inspector, both of whom she'd worked with on multiple occasions.

"She's been dead for at least twelve hours," the white-haired, bespeckled coroner told Jones. "Maybe as long as eighteen."

"What about evidence?" Jones asked a tall man wearing a blue CSI jacket.

"Looks like suicide to me," he said. "No signs of a struggle or that anyone had been in the house with her."

Jones shook her head.

"That's what I was afraid of," she said. "Thanks for getting out here so quickly."

She walked back to Fowler, standing at his car.

"Nothing left to do here," she said. "Let's go."

As they drove off, she looked back to see the two patrolmen wrapping yellow crime tape over the front door.

- 9.1 -

IT WAS MID-AFTERNOON and Eldon Watkins was on his way to meet with his client at the Stonefield City Jail. The DA, Ron Olsen, decided yesterday to share the news of Sarah Elliott's escort service with Watkins.

"If there wasn't sufficient motive to prove your client killed his wife, there is now," Olsen told the hippie-looking defense attorney.

"I've worked in the same office with Sarah Elliott for years," Watkins argued. "There's no way that woman was a prostitute."

But after seeing the evidence Fowler had gathered, Watkins had to admit there was a distinct possibility he'd been fooled by Sarah Elliott all those years. The new information about Rand Eliott's wife was not going to help his defense, and Watkins was hoping his client could successfully refute what the DA had told him. It was too important to wait until Monday.

RAND ELLIOTT had been in the same cell for more than a week. He entered the jail as a fit, healthy-looking 38-year-old, but he'd lost ten pounds over nine days. His distaste for prison food and his growing paranoia combined to shed a pound a day.

Rand's orange jumpsuit hung on his diminished frame like a blanket tossed over a fence post. His narrow face had thinned even further, forming hollow cheeks. Rand's court date was set for late October, three weeks away. If his weight loss continued at the current rate, there would be no one left to try.

No other prisoners were in the jailhouse, so Watkins agreed to meet with his client in his cell, saving the jailer from taking Elliott to the interrogation room.

Elliott was seated on the edge of his cot, bouncing a rubber ball off the floor, over and over again. The clang of the heavy metal door into the jailhouse caused him to look up. Watkins walked to Elliott's cell and stood outside, waiting for the jailer to unlock the door.

"It's been three days," Elliott said. "Where the hell've you been?"

"I've been looking for something to save you from a life in prison," Watkins replied as he stepped inside.

The jailer let the door slam behind him. Elliott and Watkins both flinched.

"Watch it with the door, you khaki-covered worm!" Elliott shouted.

"I see you're still making friends with the locals," Watkins said.

"You gotta get me outta here," Elliott pleaded. "I won't make it another three weeks."

"You better find a way to deal with this. I have news that doesn't help your case."

"What's that?"

"The DA has proof that Sarah's been operating a personal escort service."

Elliott's eyes narrowed.

"You mean she's been arranging dates for men?" he asked.

"I mean she's been selling herself to men."

Elliott stood and stepped toward Watkins.

"Take that back! Or I'll tear you apart right here in this cell."

"Settle down. The DA has a statement from one of Sarah's clients and video of her with a second man at a hotel," Watkins said. "If that isn't bad enough, I've seen her ads on her website, DearingDates.com. I'm afraid it's true."

Elliott fell back onto the cot, continuing to stare at Watkins. The look on Elliott's face already answered Watkins' next question, but he had to ask.

"Were you aware of what she was doing?"

The veins in Elliott's temples popped and his neck turned a dark crimson.

"Get out of here!" he shouted.

Watkins held up his palms toward Elliott.

"There's nothing you can do about this now. Sarah's gone. We need to figure out where to go from here."

Elliott stood and began to pace the ten-foot-long cell.

"Was she with anyone I know?" he asked.

"I'm not sure, but the client who provided a statement was from Charlotte."

"I didn't kill my wife over this," he argued, standing in front of Watkins. "I would've killed the men first."

"Sit down," Watkins ordered. "We need to create doubt in the minds of the jurors. I have a few ideas, but they need detail."

"Like what?"

"Sarah's briefcase hasn't been found. Can you think of anyone who stood to be exposed if its contents became known?"

"As far as I knew, she only kept case documents in it," Elliott replied. "But if she was running an escort service, I imagine all of her clients would fear what was in her briefcase."

"I've thought of that, but not knowing the names of her johns, it's hard to prove any of them are killers."

"What about the guy from Charlotte?"

"I checked him out. He's clean," Watkins said. "He claims he paid for her dinner, but turned down her services."

"You mentioned another guy on a video. Do you have his name?"

"Not yet. The video shows Sarah walking out of the hotel with him wearing a dark jacket. His face is not on camera."

"What else you got?" Elliott asked.

"The timeline is the other opportunity to create doubt," Watkins said. "The coroner confirmed time of death sometime between six and eight that evening. You claim to have arrived closer to nine. We need to find someone or something to support your story."

"It's not a story. It's the truth!" Elliott shouted.

"Then help me prove it. Help me find something to prove you entered your home around nine."

"Someone *had* to see me drive by the clubhouse. There are streetlights all around there, and I've got the only Tesla in the neighborhood."

"That's a good idea," Watkins said. "No one has come forward voluntarily, but if I press those who left dinner around the time you passed, I might shake their memories."

"The hostess at the club is Meg Bradley," Rand said. "She'd have the names of those dining that night as well as the time they were seated."

Watkins wrote down the name.

"It's worth a shot."

- 9.2 -

JONES AND FOWLER WERE SAFELY back at his home in Stonefield. Both had kicked off their shoes and were enjoying a beer in the living room. They'd driven the 75 miles from Charlotte still stunned and saying little. After a few minutes in the quiet of Fowler's home, their conversation picked up.

"I think it's time we get Jeremy Wilson or James Statler, the mystery CEO, to answer some questions on the record," Jones said.

"The coroner is likely to find Rose Ratcliff's death to be a suicide. There was no evidence of trauma and she left a note," Fowler said. "What crime are you going to question the MedEX execs about?"

"Malone Motts is dead from an overdose and now his girlfriend. The day before she died, she was scared to death when she handed me that warning note."

"The note wasn't very specific," Fowler said. "It didn't say what was going down, or who would die. We assume she was referring to MedEX, but Wilson would just deny any knowledge of it."

"At least we'd have him on the record," she replied. "And who knows, maybe he'd crack under the pressure and sing like a bird."

"It's possible, but not likely," Fowler said. "His life wouldn't be worth two cents if he turned in whoever's behind all this."

"Don't forget my two dead informants," she said. "And the creep who stalked me in the BMW. You've gotta believe MedEX had something to do with all that."

"I agree it all looks like MedEX is at the center of the storm, but so far, we have nothing solid to pin on anyone," Fowler replied.

"Wilson struck me as the kinda guy who would crack under pressure," Jones said. "He just took Motts' job, and I have the feeling he's in way over his head."

"That's the Peter Principle," Fowler said before taking another swig from the bottle.

"What's that?"

"Some guy named Peter developed this principle that claims people working in a hierarchical organization eventually rise to a position where they prove to be incompetent."

"Is this stuff you learned at Piedmont Community College?" Jones mocked before taking a drink. "Let's get back on point. I say we get Wilson on the record and see if he knows anything about what's going down."

"Sounds like a plan, but I doubt Pierce will approve of me getting in on that. You'll need to find your scariest interrogator to assist with the call."

"What do you mean Pierce won't approve?" she asked, frowning. "You didn't seem too concerned about Pierce when you picked a lock to break into a victim's home in Charlotte."

"I was just your driver this morning," he argued. "I don't think I should be getting any deeper in the Motts MedEX case until we find some connection to a crime committed in Stonefield."

"It sounds like your DA has closed the case on the Elliott murder," she said. "So, are you just going to coast for a while?"

"I never coast. I'm still not convinced we have all the answers on the Elliott case."

"Like what?"

"Where's Sarah's briefcase? And why would Rand take it? And I still can't believe he'd be so careless with the murder weapon."

"I agree. And you can bet Eldon Watkins will shine a bright light on all those questions," she said. "But you're outta leads. Where do you go next?"

"I'm not exactly sure. Maybe I'll take a closer look at Sarah Elliott's client list," he replied. "And the guy on the video in the dark jacket is still bugging me."

"I hate that tomorrow is Sunday," Jones said. "There's not much either of us can do."

"We need to stop by and pay our respects to Abby Jenkins on Monday," Fowler added. "And I got a text from Pierce confirming the funeral is Tuesday."

"I won't miss the funeral," Jones said. "But I have to get back to MedEX on Monday. I can't let this go any longer. You didn't see the look on Rose Ratcliff's face. I believed her when she said something is going down."

"Let's plan on visiting Abby early Monday," Fowler said. "Then we'll both get back to work."

- 9.3 -

JEREMY WILSON was at his home in east Charlotte, playing *Grand Theft Auto* on his 50-inch television. It was what he did to unwind most days. Divorced years ago, he lived alone in a modest three-bedroom home with his 9-year-old cat, Shadow.

He flipped off the game and switched the TV back to cable before going to the kitchen. It was time for a snack that usually served as his dinner. He could hear Channel 6 news in the background as he lathered mayonnaise on a turkey sandwich.

The drug epidemic plaguing this city has claimed another victim. Rose Ratcliff, age thirty-six and an employee of a local pharmaceutical company, was found dead in her home in east Charlotte earlier today. She was the apparent victim of opioid abuse.

Wilson dropped his knife and ran back to the living room in time to see a driver's license photo of Rose Ratcliff on the screen.

"Shit! What have they done?" he muttered.

He went to his computer in the den to search for anything else about Ratcliff's death, but he couldn't find anything more than what he'd heard on TV.

It was late Saturday, but he knew Jerald Jefferson rarely left his office. Jefferson had also told him on multiple occasions-- Don't call me, I'll call *you.*

Wilson paced his living room in a mental tug-of-war with himself.

I'll call him.

But he'll be furious.

I can't wait 'til Monday.

He must've done this!

About to explode, Wilson picked up his cellphone and called Jefferson's office number. He answered on the first ring.

"Jefferson here."

"It's Wilson. I just heard about Rose Ratcliff. What the hell happened?"

"I just learned the news myself."

"I thought your guys were just going to talk to her-- straighten her out."

"And that's exactly what they did," Jefferson said. "They took her home, she had a soda, and my guys had a long talk about her future at MedEX."

"Well, she's dead. And your guys were the last to see her. It doesn't look good."

"Settle down, Wilson. No one will know who was with her. My guys are good about cleaning up after themselves."

"So, they *did* kill her," he said, his hands shaking.

"No. That's not what I said, and you can't even think that."

"That female cop was just at MedEX asking about Motts," Wilson said. "You know she's going to assume the worst about Ratcliff."

"Wilson, stay calm. It's not unusual for couples to have problems that lead to bad decisions, despair, and even death. And that's exactly what happened with Motts and Ratcliff."

Jefferson was attempting to be soft-spoken and reassuring, but it was impossible to wring the evil out of his voice.

"I want to believe you."

"You must believe me. It's the only way."

Wilson continued to pace, his forehead and armpits damp with sweat.

"Maybe *you* should talk to the cops when they return. I know they're coming back," Wilson pleaded. "That woman detective asked about Mr. Statler. She's going to demand to see the CEO."

"You're the site manager now. The buck at MedEX stops with you," Jefferson said, his voice firm. "You and I both know Mr. Statler exists only on paper. I sign his documents, but I don't make his appearances. You do."

Wilson was silent. He stepped to his picture window and stared out at a darkening sky. There was nowhere for him to go.

"You can handle this, Wilson. You *must* handle it."

The line went silent.

- Day 10 -
Sunday

IT WAS THE 21st CENTURY, but Eldon Watkins, the grey-haired, ponytailed 68-year-old attorney, would have been at home in San Francisco's Haight-Ashbury district during the 1960's—and so would his home.

Comfort ruled the décor of Watkins' midcentury modern house, complete with beanbag chairs and a futon in the living room. A thick sheepskin rug that came to your ankles occupied the space in front of his brick fireplace. He'd even framed a favorite tie-dyed shirt from college and hung it in the hallway. His ex-wife had tried several times to toss the shirt out, but each time, he rescued it before trash pickup.

Watkins had found Sarah Elliott to be not only a qualified attorney, but also a kindred spirit, compatible with his thoughts and ideology. The proof of her running a personal escort service had yet to fully sink in, but there was no denying the evidence. The only explanation he could muster was that after years of defending the poor and wrongly accused, and putting up with her husband's antics, she must've wanted more.

As Watkins relaxed to a jazz medley on his turntable, he sipped a cappuccino. He'd just concocted the drink from a machine resembling something from a Jules Verne science adventure film. He leaned back in a sagging leather chair that faced a window out to his backyard.

His brown and white, mixed breed spaniel, Maggie, lay near his feet. They often talked to each other, but only Maggie could understand what the other was saying.

"I'm beginning to think I'm gettin' too old for this, girl," he said, causing Maggie to raise her head. She looked up with attentive brown eyes focused on her master's expression.

"We're both about the same age, but it's taken me a hell of a lot longer to get here. You'd think I'd be smarter by now."

Watkins gazed out the back window and resumed sipping his cappuccino. Maggie returned her head to the floor.

"I've got an innocent man depending on me, and I'm not sure I got the energy or smarts to fight off the thirty-somethings who're out to get him."

Maggie rose to her feet and circled around in front of Watkins. She sat on her haunches and stared at him as if to say-- *Go ahead. Get it all out.*

Watkins smiled.

"I'm ruining the music, aren't I, Maggie?" he said, bending down to rub her floppy ears. "I'll be quiet for a while, but then I need to get my ass in gear. There are some folks at Stonefield Estates I need to go see."

MEG BRADLEY, the longtime hostess at the Stonefield Estates Country Club, had just finished the Sunday brunch shift when Watkins entered the lobby.

Families dressed in their church attire slowly filed out, many turning to look at the eccentric attorney as he approached the hostess stand. Watkins had added a tie and white shirt to his corduroy jacket in an effort to blend in. It wasn't working.

A stately woman with silver hair wearing a simple black dress stood behind a tall, narrow podium. She turned the page in her hostess book listing brunch reservations and glanced over the page for Sunday's lunch guests.

"Hi, ma'am. Are you Ms. Bradley?"

"Yes. How may I help you?" she asked, looking at Watkins like he was stealing silverware.

"I'm Eldon Watkins. I called yesterday regarding information about your dinner guests from a week ago Friday."

"Yes, Mr. Watkins. I remember."

"Do you have time to talk now?" he asked.

"For a few minutes," she replied. "There's an office around the corner."

Watkins followed her into a small, wood-paneled room. A desk with two cushioned side chairs were its only furnishings. Bradley closed the door behind them, but continued to stand.

"Can you tell me exactly what you're requesting?" she asked.

"Rand Elliott is my client. I'm looking for anyone who may have seen his car pass the clubhouse between eight-thirty and nine a week ago from this past Friday. Determining the time that he drove past is critical to his defense."

"And you think I can assist you with this?"

"I'm assuming you have a record of the reservations for that night and the time the diners were seated."

"Yes, I'm sure I can find my reservation sheet for that night."

"How long does it usually take for your members to eat dinner and be on their way?"

"It's hard to say," she replied, crossing her arms. "We don't hurry our club members. On a Friday night, some might take three hours, others are in and out in ninety minutes or less."

Watkins used his fingers to do some quick math.

"Backing up from nine o'clock, I'd like to get a list of the patrons seated between six and seven-thirty."

"That would be most of the dinner crowd that night— probably eighty people or more," she replied. "I'd have to discuss this with Mr. Dorsey, the club manager, before I provide the names of that many members."

Watkins thought.

"Were you working that night?" he asked.

"Yes, I work most weekends, Friday through Sunday."

"Were you at the hostess stand as late as nine?"

"Probably. We stop serving at eight, but I stick around longer."

"Is it possible you could look at the reservations from that night and identify those who left later in the evening?"

"Maybe a few, but my list wouldn't be totally accurate or complete."

"I'll take what you can provide now," he said. "If I need more names, I'll come back later."

"You want these names *now*?" she asked, becoming irritated.

"Please. Whatever you can provide."

Bradley's eyes narrowed.

"Mr. Watkins, if it were up to me, I'd refuse your request. I think Rand Elliott should pay for what he did to that beautiful woman."

"Mr. Elliott hasn't been convicted. He's only been accused," Watkins replied. "I assume you're an advocate of fair trials."

She pressed her lips thin with anger.

"Please wait in the lobby," she huffed. "I'll speak with Mr. Dorsey and get back with you."

WATKINS FOUND a comfortable chair in the lobby and checked his email on his cellphone.

"Aren't you the attorney who shared office space with Sarah Elliott?"

The question came from a smiling, dark-haired woman wearing a flowing black dress and a white wrap around her shoulders.

Watkins stood.

"Yes, I'm Eldon Watkins and Sarah did share space with me," he replied. "I'm afraid I've forgotten your name."

"We only met briefly," the pleasant 50-year-old replied. "I'm Joan Felton. Sarah and I were downtown shopping last fall and stopped by your office."

"You must have a good memory," he said.

"You're pretty easy to remember."

"I *am* rather handsome," he kidded.

Mrs. Felton smiled.

"I was surprised to hear you're defending Rand," she said, "especially knowing Sarah as well as you did."

"We were good friends. I miss her already," he said.

"You must think Rand is innocent to take his case."

"I do. In fact, I'm convinced of it."

"What brings you to our club today?"

"I'm interested in who dined here the night of the murder," he replied. "I'm looking for someone who might have seen Rand Elliott's silver Tesla pass by around nine."

"My husband and I ate here that night," she replied. "In fact, the Elliotts were supposed to join us. Maybe if they had, none of this would've happened."

"It'll drive you crazy to consider what might've changed the past," he said.

"I thought I saw Rand's car pass that night," Mrs. Felton said. "But I'd had a couple Chardonnays, and my husband convinced me it wasn't a Tesla."

"What time would that have been?"

"It was after eight-thirty," she replied. "I remember because the nine o'clock news was coming on when we got home."

"So, you saw a silver car go by, but your husband said it wasn't a Tesla?"

"That's right. He knows a lot more about cars than I do."

"Is he here at the club this morning?"

"No, he's traveling this weekend, attending a medical conference in Dallas."

"Were either of you contacted by police about the Elliott murder?"

"Yeah, we talked to an officer that night and then again to detectives the next day."

"And you didn't mention seeing a silver car?"

"We saw a silver car, but Stan was certain it wasn't Rand's."

"Do you happen to remember if anyone was leaving at the same time you were?" Watkins asked.

She paused.

"I think Carl and Linda Johnson were in the car in front of us," she said. "They turned the other direction as we approached the stop sign."

"Before or after the silver car passed?"

"Before, I'm pretty sure."

Meg Bradley approached with a single sheet of paper in her hand.

"Hello, Mrs. Felton. I hope you're having a good morning," Bradley said, smiling.

"I am, thanks. But I need to be going," she said before heading toward the exit. "It was good to see you again, Mr. Watkins."

Bradley handed the sheet of paper to Watkins.

"Here are ten names. I'm pretty sure they all left after eight-thirty that night."

He glanced at the list. The Feltons and Johnsons were included.

"Thank you," he said, folding the paper and sticking it inside his coat pocket.

- 10.1 -

THE SUNDAY LUNCH CROWD at the Stonefield Cracker Barrel spilled out onto the front porch. It had taken 20 minutes for Jones and Fowler to work their way to the top of the queue. They now waited inside near the cash register.

"You actually like eating here?" Jones asked. "I always feel like I'm with refugees waiting to board a ship to freedom."

Fowler chuckled.

"I bet the ship to freedom didn't have chicken and dumplings like this place," he replied.

A moment later, they followed a teenaged girl with blue streaks in her hair and holding a stack of menus to a high-back wooden booth.

"You doing the buffet or ordering off the menu?" the server asked as they slid across from each other.

Jones glanced over her shoulder to the chaos at the buffet.

"Menu, please," she replied.

They quickly read over the multi-page menu and ordered.

"You were on your computer a long time this morning," Jones said. "Anything new?"

"I asked SBI Forensics for text records from the cell number used by Sarah Elliott. It turns out she used an encrypted text service that immediately erased conversations."

"Could you at least get the cell numbers of her escort clients?" she asked.

"She had many clients contact her over the most recent six-month period, but only a few with multiple interactions," Fowler replied. "I'm assuming the others either got cold feet or were scared away by her fees."

"Was she expensive?"

"You don't want to know," Fowler replied.

"Is that it then? Nothing else to pursue relating to her scummy escort clients?"

"Forensics is looking into the numbers with multiple contacts. So far, they've hit dead ends. Most of her clients' phones are unregistered or unlisted."

"I'm sure there were other contacts those guys wanted to keep private," Jones scoffed.

The waitress brought their drinks, and they quickly paused their discussion.

"I really don't want to get anyone other than you involved in my meeting at MedEX tomorrow," Jones said, lowering her voice and leaning closer. "First of all, I don't even know if Lieutenant Alvarez has anyone available to go with me."

"I could talk to Pierce about going, but he's been clear about me staying on the Elliott case."

"I can't believe your DA and chief are being so closed-minded about this," she said. "Sarah Elliott was defending Malone Motts, the former site manager at MedEX. What more of a connection do they need?"

"We have a murder weapon with Rand's fingerprints. Pierce and Olsen consider the case closed, if for no other reason, to calm the public."

"Working with me to investigate MedEX shouldn't upset the public."

"I agree, but for Pierce to agree, we still need evidence tying the two cases together."

Fowler's cellphone interrupted their conversation. It was Eldon Watkins.

"Can you talk?" Watkins asked.

"I'm at lunch. Is it urgent?"

"I've found a witness who says she saw Elliott pass the clubhouse near nine o'clock."

"Who's that?"

"Joan Felton."

"I've talked to the Feltons. They said they didn't see Rand Elliott that night," Fowler replied.

"Joan Felton saw a silver sedan and was sure it was Rand Elliott, but her husband was convinced it wasn't a Tesla."

"Did she recognize Rand in the car?"

"No, but she saw a man driving a silver car."

"If the Feltons disagree on what they saw, you really don't have a witness," Fowler said.

"Maybe. Maybe not. I've found a tie-breaker."

"Who's that?"

"The Johnsons pulled out of the clubhouse immediately before Joan and Stan Felton," he replied. "They must've seen the silver Tesla."

"Have you spoken to them?"

"Not yet. They're in Costa Rica and not returning until next weekend. Their voicemail says their phone service will be intermittent and they'll return calls as available."

"What do you want me to do?" Fowler asked.

"I've left a message for the Johnsons, but thought you could pay another call on the Feltons," Watkins replied. "According to his wife, Stan Felton is out of town, returning Tuesday."

"It would help if you talked to the Johnsons before I bother the Feltons again," Fowler said.

"I'll let you know as soon as I do."

Fowler stuffed his phone back into his pocket.

"What was that all about?" Jones asked.

"Maybe nothing," Fowler said. "Or maybe the Elliott murder case is about to open up again."

- Day 11 -
Monday

THE MECKLENBURG COUNTY Coroner's toxicology report came back as expected. Rose Ratcliff died from ingesting a lethal dose of opioids. Given her suicide note and lack of evidence indicating foul play, her death was ruled a suicide.

"I saw Rose the day before she died," Jones said after reading the report on Fowler's computer. "I can't believe there was no consideration given to my statement or to the note she gave me."

"The coroner has to go with physical evidence," Fowler said. "You know that."

"The note *is* physical evidence!" she argued.

"I agree with you, but the note wasn't very specific."

Fowler and Jones moved to the kitchen, but neither felt like eating breakfast. They drank black coffee and nibbled on bagels as they readied for a day of emotion and uncertainty.

"I'm not good with grief," Jones said, still sipping her first cup of coffee. "I never know what to say to someone who just lost a family member."

"Just being there provides comfort," Fowler replied. "I don't remember what anyone said at my mom's funeral, but I remember who was there."

"What time is Abby expecting us?"

"Pierce said she and her son will be busy with funeral preparation this morning, and it would be best to catch them around nine," Fowler replied.

"I'm gonna call Alvarez and let him know that I'm going back to MedEX later today to question Jeremy Wilson," she said. "Should I ask about lining up a partner to go with me, or is there a chance you'll be able to go?"

"I'm headed into the station to talk with Pierce this morning," he replied. "I need to let him know about the possibility of Watkins finding someone to confirm Rand Elliott's alibi. It might make a difference in him agreeing to let me work the Motts case."

"Do you think Watkins is really onto something?" she asked.

"Hard to tell, but if he validates Elliott's alibi, it will open up Sarah's murder to other suspects, including those close to Motts or possibly one of Sarah's escorts."

"Maybe Sarah knew what was going down at MedEX, and that's what got her killed," Jones said.

"That's a stretch," Fowler replied. "I keep thinking about what you and the inmate in Asheville told me."

"What's that?"

"That stabbings are usually personal, and that professional killers don't like to leave a trail of evidence behind."

"The deaths of the others linked to MedEX would support that theory," Jones said. "My informants were gunned down by pros, and Motts and his girlfriend died of overdoses. I'd be willing to bet they were all at the hands of experienced killers."

"No doubt the hit on your informants was a professional job," Fowler said. "It's gonna be tougher to link the two overdoses to anyone, or to even prove they were murders."

Fowler tipped back the rest of his coffee.

"I better go see Pierce if we're going to make it to Abby's by nine."

"I'll be ready when you get back," she replied. "Good luck."

CHIEF PIERCE was on his phone when Fowler arrived at the police station, so he continued to his cubicle in the detectives' bullpen.

The makeshift memorial at Brooks Jenkins' cubicle had exploded over the weekend. Flowers and cards covered the detective's desk and surrounded his chair, extending down the aisle. Fowler noticed cards from former officers and detectives who'd retired years ago.

They must've come in over the weekend, he thought as he read several of the posted notes.

For a long moment, Fowler stared at the outpouring of love and respect for his fallen partner. A lump returned to his throat.

There now was an opening on senior detective row. Fowler was next in line to move to a desk along the wall of windows, but it no longer mattered to him.

I could never take Jenkins' desk, he thought.

Seated at his cubicle, Fowler quickly sorted through the interoffice mail and notes that had accumulated. Nothing required his immediate attention, so he stacked the papers on the corner of his desk.

His cellphone rang as he rose to go see Pierce. It was Eldon Watkins.

"You're at work early," Fowler answered.

"I heard back from Carl Johnson last night. He said he and his wife didn't know Rand Elliott, nor would they recognize his car."

"So, your lead was a dead end?" Fowler asked.

"To the contrary. He remembered leaving the clubhouse that night and driving out of the parking lot just ahead of Dr. and Mrs. Felton."

"Did he see Elliott's car or not?"

"Johnson said he turned left in front of an oncoming car. It was silver and going faster than he thought. He recalled his wife telling him that he should've waited for it to pass."

"This is all interesting, and a testament to Mr. Johnson's memory, but if he didn't know Elliott or what kinda car he drove, it has no bearing on Elliott's alibi."

"His wife remembers the vanity plate on the front of the car that sped past them," Watkins said. "It was in a chrome frame and read: JUST4ME."

Fowler's eyes widened. He'd seen the vanity plate on the silver Tesla in Rand's garage.

"She's sure about this?" Fowler asked.

"She's willing to provide a sworn statement including the time she saw the car pass," Watkins replied. "And Mrs. Felton has already confirmed she and her husband left at the same time, shortly before nine."

"But Dr. Felton swore it wasn't a Tesla," Fowler argued.

"He must not know his cars as well as he thought he did. Turns out Mrs. Felton was right about the car belonging to Elliott."

"We still have a murder weapon with your client's prints," Fowler said. "I doubt this new information will be enough for the DA to drop charges, and maybe the coroner missed Sarah's exact time of death."

"You can chase that theory down a rabbit hole if you wish, but we both know Doc Richards doesn't make those kinda mistakes," Watkins argued. "As soon as I get the Johnsons' statements, I'll be moving for the charges against Elliott to be dropped."

The line went dead. Fowler lowered his cellphone to his lap and sat thinking about what he'd just heard. He stuffed the phone into his coat pocket and went to see Chief Pierce.

Pierce was at his desk reviewing weekend reports. He looked up when he heard a rap at the door.

"Are you here to fill me in on what happened in Charlotte Saturday?" Pierce asked.

"I left you a voicemail," Fowler replied. "I drove Detective Jones to MedEX to follow up on a disturbing note she'd received from Rose Ratcliff the day before. Turns out we were too late."

"The report I got from CMPD this morning says you broke into Ratcliff's home."

"We had reason to believe she was in danger, so I picked the door lock," he replied. "Once Detective Jones verified Ratcliff was dead, she immediately called CMPD."

"I heard it was suicide."

"Possibly, but I doubt it," Fowler replied.

"Just the same, don't be making any more trips to Charlotte to investigate MedEX or Motts without me knowing."

"That's the main reason I'm here," Fowler said. "I just talked to Watkins. He's convinced he has witnesses who will corroborate Elliott's alibi."

"What? Is he serious?"

"I believe so," Fowler replied. "He's talked to Carl Johnson, a member of the club at Stonefield Estates. He and his wife finished dinner shortly before nine and saw a silver car pass them going the other direction."

"Why didn't they come forward before now?"

"They didn't know it was Rand Elliott. In fact, they don't know him at all."

"So, how do they know it was Elliott who passed them that night?"

"Mrs. Johnson remembers the vanity plate on Rand Elliott's car."

"Have you talked to the Johnsons?"

"Not yet. They're in Costa Rica until this weekend," Fowler replied. "Jenkins and I did talk to Dr. Felton and his wife who left the clubhouse at the same time as the Johnsons that night."

"Did they see Elliott?"

"They told us they saw a silver car, but Dr. Felton was sure it wasn't a Tesla."

"What about his wife?"

"She's now telling Watkins that it *was* Elliott, but she didn't say anything to me and Jenkins because her husband talked her out of it."

"I assume Watkins is going to move for the charges to be dismissed?"

"Yeah. As soon as he gets a sworn statement from Mrs. Johnson, he said he'd contact the DA's office."

"Sounds like the shit's gonna hit the fan this weekend," Pierce said.

"I think it would be a good idea to continue pursuing the Motts connection to Sarah Elliott's death," Fowler said.

"Help me with that logic," Pierce replied.

"There are several recent deaths involving people connected to MedEX, Rose Ratcliff being the latest," Fowler began. "It wouldn't be surprising if Sarah Elliott's death is another linked to Motts and MedEX."

"We have no evidence indicating either MedEX or Motts are involved," Pierce argued. "On the other hand, we have proof that Rand Elliott committed that murder. Don't forget about the knife."

"I don't know how, but I've always thought that was staged," Fowler replied.

"Are you suggesting someone put Rand's prints on a knife and then stabbed his wife with it?"

"I bet you have prints on knives at your house," Fowler said. "What if I picked one up while wearing gloves and stabbed someone with it?"

"Where's the evidence to support that wild idea?" Pierce asked, tossing his hands into the air.

"The murder weapon was a steak knife matching others from the Elliotts' home."

"I would assume that was the closest knife for Elliott to use," Pierce said. "You admitted that stabbings are an act of passion. Elliott likely became enraged, found the knife in his kitchen, and killed his wife."

"I agree that's a reasonable scenario. I'm just saying there are other possibilities we haven't considered. Now that Watkins has found someone to support Rand Elliott's alibi, we may need to broaden our search for suspects."

Pierce blew out a long breath and leaned forward with his forearms on his desk.

"Let me guess. You want to work the Motts case with Detective Jones."

"I think all these deaths, including Sarah Elliott's, are linked to Malone Motts and something that's going on at MedEX."

"What's your next step?" Pierce asked.

"After we pay a visit on Abby Jenkins and her son this morning, Jones and I are going back to Charlotte to talk with the site manager."

Pierce paused, staring up at Fowler.

"Keep me informed."

- 11.1 -

FOWLER PULLED his cruiser to the curb in front of a two-story, white Victorian. The home was immaculately maintained and set on a rise above the road with steps leading up to a wide, covered porch.

Brooks and Abby Jenkins had lived on the tree-lined street since their wedding day thirty years ago. The century-old home had been in Abby's family for several generations, passing to her and Brooks after her father died at a young age from a heart attack. Prior to the death of Abby's mother, she lived in the home with Brooks, Abby, and their son, Kerry.

Fowler had been to the house only once to pick up a police report from Detective Jenkins. On that visit, he'd not gone past the porch.

Jones and Fowler walked side-by-side up the steps. She was dressed in a black pantsuit and white blouse. Fowler had added a tie to this blue sport coat and grey slacks. He carried an apple pie they'd just purchased at a downtown bakery.

"You do the talking," Jones said nervously as they reached the arching wood door.

"You'll be fine," he replied.

He knocked lightly three times. Seconds later, footsteps moved quickly toward them from the other side, and the door swung open.

A younger version of Brooks Jenkins stood before them. Over six feet tall, Kerry was solidly built and had a kind face like his father.

Kerry's eyes went first to Jones and then to Fowler.

"I'm Jack Fowler. I was your father's partner, and this is Angela Jones. She's a Charlotte detective and a friend of your dad's. We're so sorry for your loss. Your father will be missed by this entire community."

"Thank you. Mom tells me that he spoke highly of you, as well. Please step inside. She'll be glad to see you."

Kerry accepted the pie from Jack and set it on a table in the hallway before leading them to a formal sitting room decorated with period furnishings. His mother sat in a wingback chair before a cozy fireplace, wearing a long black skirt and a dark shawl around her shoulders. Her thick, white hair was neatly gathered behind her head. Funeral brochures and other documents were scattered over the coffee table in front of her.

"Thanks for coming," Abby greeted, rising from her chair.

"This is Angela Jones," Jack said. "She and your husband met a couple of times when Angela was working a case here in Stonefield."

Abby stepped closer and extended her hand to Angela.

"He mentioned you to me. You are even more beautiful than Brooks described."

Angela smiled.

"Your husband was an inspiration to me and many others, Mrs. Jenkins. I'm so sorry for your loss."

"Thank you, dear. Kerry and I are still in denial, but Brooks would want us to move on, so we're doing our best."

"I hope Chief Pierce asked you about being a pallbearer tomorrow," Abby said.

"Yes, he did. Angela and I would be glad to help in any way possible," Jack replied.

Abby glanced down at the documents and brochures scattered on the table.

"Everything is so overwhelming, but it's slowly coming together," she said. "And in a way, it's helping to keep my mind busy. It's the quiet moments that are the worst."

"We need to be in Charlotte today," Angela said. "But please let us know if there's anything you need for tomorrow."

"There *is* one thing," Abby said. "Brooks and I have a small family. He and I would be proud if you two would sit with us."

"We'd be honored, but are you sure?" Jack asked.

"I'm positive. Your dad gave Brooks the chance to become a detective, the first black detective on the SPD force. Brooks never forgot that."

Turning to Angela, she said, "You may not realize it, but you made a big impression on my husband, too. I don't know what you told him when you met, but it clearly lifted his spirits."

"I just told him the truth," Angela said. "That he was a leader for me and others to follow."

Abby stepped forward, rested her hands on Angela's shoulders, and gave her a kiss on the cheek.

"Bless you," she said.

"Mrs. Jenkins, please call us if you need anything," Jack offered again, inching toward the hall. "Angela and I should be on our way and let you and Kerry prepare for tomorrow."

"Yes," Abby said, a resolve coming to her face. "The service must be a proper tribute to Brooks."

"I'm sure it will be," Angela said.

Abby walked her guests to the front door.

"Be safe today and always."

"I'M A LITTLE STUNNED," Fowler said, descending the steps toward his car. "I never knew Jenkins considered me family. I barely talked to him before we became partners."

"She was sincere," Jones replied. "It's clear he respected you and your father."

"Did you feel a connection with Jenkins when you met him?" Fowler asked.

"Yeah. I could see my father in him," she replied. "And I could sense the pressure that he was under to perform."

"To perform?" he asked.

"It's hard to explain, Jack, but being the first at anything, you feel like you're being measured, maybe even a little unfairly. Still, you don't want to blow the opportunity."

"I never thought about it that way," he replied. "Too bad Jenkins didn't get the chance to solve his first murder case."

"He started the investigation with you," Jones said. "We need to make sure we finish it."

- 11.2 -

JONES REQUESTED a warrant to search the office of Jeremy Wilson, Rose Ratcliff's manager and the new site executive at MedEX Pharmaceuticals. Her request was immediately denied by a Mecklenburg County magistrate, citing insufficient evidence of wrongdoing in Ratcliff's death.

With the deaths of Motts and Ratcliff ruled suicides, the only crime that Jones could use to compel Wilson's testimony was the double murder of Jones' informants. But Jones didn't want to take the time to have a subpoena issued.

The better option was for Jones and Fowler to call Wilson's bluff. They'd tell him he could answer questions regarding Ratcliff's death in his office, or he could come down to CMPD headquarters to be questioned. The detectives knew his cooperation would be voluntary, but there was no reason to tell Wilson.

JONES AND FOWLER waited on the sidewalk outside MedEX Pharmaceuticals for the next employee to enter the lobby. Minutes later, a man in his 40s wearing a white lab coat approached the entrance. They quickly moved forward and flashed their badges.

"We're here to see Jeremy Wilson," Jones said, "and hoping you can let us inside."

"Is he expecting you?" the man asked.

"No," she replied. "But I met with him last Friday, and this is a follow-up."

"Wait in the lobby. This could take a while, but I'll see what I can do," he said, before disappearing through a door leading to a long hallway.

After reaching the lab, the man in the white coat called security who, in turn, contacted Wilson in his office.

"The two detectives I spoke with over the weekend are in the lobby waiting to see you," the stocky security guard reported. "They say it's a follow-up to the meeting the female cop had with you last Friday."

Wilson fidgeted with a pen on his desk as he thought.

"Bring them to my office and wait outside while they're here."

"Are you expecting trouble?" the guard asked, seemingly excited about that prospect.

"No, but I'd feel better knowing you're available to escort them out at any time."

"I'll be there in a couple minutes."

The guard with tattooed forearms and a military crew cut appeared in the lobby. With little discussion, he instructed Jones and Fowler to follow him to Wilson's office. They proceeded through a labyrinth of long corridors to the far corner of the building.

The site manager's office presented the same unsuccessful vibe as the MedEX lobby. The chrome accented furniture and shelves were out of the 1970s. A wall of windows behind Wilson's desk overlooked a two-acre grassy area with a man-made pond outlined with decorative rocks and tall grasses. Water shot skyward in a circular pattern from the pond's center, adding modest interest to what otherwise was an artificial-looking backdrop. If the company was making money, it didn't appear any of it was being reinvested into the facility or its grounds.

Wilson stood as they entered, pushing his Clark Kent-style glasses off his nose and back to his face.

"I'll be right outside, Mr. Wilson," the guard said, glancing at the detectives with a warning glare.

"Detective Jones, I thought we covered everything last Friday," Wilson said. "And I really don't have time today for you and your friend."

"I'm Detective Fowler," he said, stepping forward and sticking his badge inches from Wilson's face. "Detective Jones and I are investigating a string of deaths that appear to be linked to your company."

Wilson recoiled, looking at Fowler like a schoolboy about to be pummeled with a dodgeball.

"Like I told you, I'm short on time today," he said, nervously gathering papers from his desk.

Fowler moved closer, his legs bumping the desk, rattling pencils jutting from a MedEX logo coffee mug.

"I suggest you talk with us now, or we'll get a subpoena for you to come downtown," Fowler warned. "The CMPD interrogation room is much smaller than this office, and you'll be on our clock there."

Wilson didn't look up. He continued to shuffle papers, putting them into a single stack.

"You're wasting your time," Wilson said. "I know nothing about a string of deaths."

Jones stepped beside her partner and slapped a strip of paper on the desk in front of Wilson.

"Maybe this note will refresh your memory. Rose Ratcliff gave it to me the day before we found her dead."

He picked up the note. As he read it, he dropped back onto his chair.

"You said Rose gave this to you?"

"That's right. She was too scared to tell me what it meant while at work," Jones said. "And Detective Fowler and I found her dead in her living room twenty-four hours later."

Wilson returned the note to the table and took a deep breath.

"She obviously wasn't of sound mind, unable to deal with her boyfriend's suicide," he said.

Fowler and Jones took seats across from Wilson.

"She wrote that something was going down and people may die. What was she talking about?" Jones asked.

"Listen. I just took this job as site manager. Until last week, I was in charge of distribution. I just shipped what we make here," Wilson said. "That's all I did. I've heard nothing about anything going down."

Fowler leaned forward to the edge of his seat, his glare burning a hole through the MedEX manager.

"Let me draw a picture for you," he began. "Malone Motts' defense attorney was found stabbed to death in her bedroom ten days ago. Less than a day later, Motts was discovered dead in his jail cell. Detective Jones arranged a meeting with two men willing to tell her what they knew about Motts, and these men were ambushed on the way to that meeting and riddled with bullets. And now, Rose Ratcliff was found dead after delivering this note to Detective Jones. That's five deaths--all the victims having links to your company."

Wilson pushed his chair away from the desk and stood.

"Sounds to me like they have links to Malone Motts, not to MedEX," he replied dismissively.

Fowler jumped to his feet and leaned forward with the palms of his hands planted on Wilson's desk.

"We're going to get to the bottom of these deaths, and when we do, those not cooperating will not fare well!"

"James!" Wilson called. "Escort the detectives to the lobby!"

The guard sprang into the office. Fowler ignored him, keeping his stare focused on Wilson, who backed away, cowering closer to the window.

"You don't strike me as the kinda guy who'd do well in federal prison," Fowler said.

"Come on, Mister," the guard interrupted, grabbing Fowler's wrist. "It's time for you to leave."

"Get your hands off of me!" Fowler shouted, pulling his hand free and shoving the guard.

The thick-necked man exploded. He reared his arm back and took a swing at Fowler's face. Fowler caught the guard's beefy hand like a third baseman snaring a line drive. He twisted the tattooed arm around to the guard's back and slammed his face against the office wall, sending framed pictures crashing to the floor.

"We know our way out," Fowler spit through his clenched jaw. "And don't you *ever* touch me again."

When Fowler released his hold, the dazed security guard slid down the wall, his knees hitting the floor with a thud. Wilson stood motionless against the window, his eyes wide and mouth agape.

"You might want to notify your boss about our visit today," Fowler told Wilson. "And while you're at it, think of better answers for the next time we come."

He pulled a business card from his jacket and tossed it onto Wilson's desk.

"Write your and your boss's phone numbers on the back."

Wilson picked up the card and stared at it.

"I'll give you my office number, but Mr. Statler doesn't give his to anyone."

Wilson jotted his number on the back and returned the card to Fowler.

"You tell Mr. Statler we plan to meet with him. It may take a few days, but we'll return with an investigative subpoena issued by a judge."

Jones and Fowler stepped from the office and wound their way back to the lobby. Fowler glanced at a security camera perched over the front doors as he exited the building.

"I'm not sure all that drama was necessary," Jones said as they reached Fowler's vehicle.

"The guard was a jerk, and Wilson now knows we mean business," he replied.

"Wilson tries to talk tough, but he reacts like a frightened sparrow," Jones said. "He's definitely hiding something, but he can't possibly be the brains behind whatever's going down."

"It sure as hell isn't Malone Motts," Fowler replied. "He's dead."

"Looks like it's time to find James Statler."

- 11.3 -

JONES AND FOWLER stopped by the SBI district office to request Lt. Alvarez's support in getting the investigative subpoena issued for James Statler's testimony. After an hour of filling out paperwork, they proceeded to Jones' home to pick up proper funeral attire for Angela. She then followed Fowler back to Stonefield.

FOWLER WENT TO HIS COMPUTER in the den with a beer and slice of pizza. Using a variety of queries, he looked for information on James Statler, but he was finding very little.

"For being the CEO and majority owner of a multi-million-dollar pharmaceutical business, there isn't much out there on this guy," Fowler said.

"Other than on the MedEX website, I didn't find much either," Jones replied as she ate her pizza over a coffee table across the room. "He didn't show up on our state and federal database at work—not even a traffic violation."

"His bio on the MedEX website is word-for-word the same as his Wikipedia page," Fowler said. "It's gotta be a cut and paste job. Neither mentions where he graduated from college, past employers, or anything about his family. It's all lofty business jargon and mentions awards he's earned—most I've never heard of."

"MedEX is a privately held company," Jones said. "I guess Statler prefers to stay out of the public eye."

"Or he's hiding something."

Fowler took another bite of pizza and pulled up the video clip from the Vista View Inn.

"The video of this guy standing behind Sarah Elliott has been bugging me ever since I first saw it," Fowler said.

He switched the video to full screen and played it again.

"I know I've seen him somewhere. He's always pulling on his sleeves as if ants are crawling up his arms."

"Too bad we can't see more of his face," Jones said. "Maybe something will come to you later."

As Fowler reached to turn off the computer, he froze, staring at the screen.

"What is it, Jack?"

"I think I know where I've seen that guy!" he said. "Or at least where I've seen those tics."

"Where?"

"Dr. Felton. When we met with him and his wife, he'd just returned from a run. I remember that he was constantly pulling at his jogging suit as if it didn't fit."

"Are you sure?" Jones asked.

"I'm sure the tics are the same, but without seeing his face, there's no way I can verify it's him."

He cycled through the video clip again and again, looking for something that supported his suspicion.

"There's nothing here to confirm it's Felton, but then, there's nothing that rules him out, either," Fowler said. "His hair is dark and there's some greying, although less greying than I remember. The height is similar, but he looked a little heavier in a jogging suit."

"Doesn't sound like you're totally convinced it's him," Jones said.

"I'm pretty sure it is."

"Enough to confront him about being with Sarah Elliott?"

"I'll have to think about that," Fowler said. "But I'd already planned to challenge him on why he was so sure the silver car he saw the night of the murder didn't belong to Rand Elliott, especially now that his wife and the Johnsons believe otherwise."

"That *is* odd."

"Felton is out of town until tomorrow, and I want to see his face when I question him. I might be able to figure out if this is him from his reactions."

"You're gonna need to stop short of accusing Felton of any wrongdoing," Jones said. "All you have is circumstantial evidence, and it's shaky at that."

"I'm just looking for his reaction, not a confession," Fowler replied. "We'll head out there after the funeral tomorrow."

- Day 12 -
Tuesday

THE SERVICE FOR BROOKS JENKINS was to be held at the First Methodist Church in Stonefield. It had been the Jenkins' family place of worship through several generations.

Forty-five minutes before the funeral was to commence, it became obvious the redbrick church with its towering steeple would not hold the hundreds of people who wished to pay their respects.

The unseasonably warm and sunny morning allowed rows of chairs to extend out the front of the church and along both sides of the sidewalk leading to the wide double-door entrance. With both doors open, the service could be heard, but not fully seen, by the overflow crowd seated on the front lawn.

Once everyone was in place, the organ played softly in the background. The pallbearers carried the casket, taking rhythmic steps, from the black hearse at the front of the church, through the double doors, and down the wide aisle to the altar. Once centered before the congregation, a blanket of white roses was placed atop the casket with vases of flowers on either side.

The pallbearers took seats near the front, with Jack sitting next to Angela in the second row, directly behind Abby and her son. Abby was dressed in black and wearing a round silk hat with a veil that extended just below her eyes. She was surrounded by neighbors and friends whom she'd asked to sit with her and Kerry.

Abby held a white handkerchief in her right hand, not needing it until Brooks' casket was placed before her. She dabbed her eyes beneath the veil repeatedly as she waited for the service to begin.

Reverend Miller stepped to the lectern cloaked in a dark purple robe with a majestic black and yellow sash. A tall, wide-shouldered man with silver hair and beard, he seemed larger than life beside the altar.

In a deep, pulsating voice, he first addressed the family, expressing his sorrow, but quickly noting the outpouring of support and the comfort such a turnout must bring to Abby and her son. He then spoke about living a life bigger than oneself. He told of how Brooks Jenkins led others, not only through his words, but through his deeds.

The pastor closed with, "Brooks Jenkins loved and worshipped God as he loved his family and the citizens of this town. May he rest in peace."

Sniffles could be heard throughout the congregation as the reverend stepped aside for Chief Pierce to deliver the eulogy.

A tear ran down Angela's cheek, and she patted it with a Kleenex. Jack reached for her hand and held it as Pierce approached the podium.

Pierce took a deep breath and placed his notes on the lectern. He was stoic and in control of his emotions. He'd known Brooks and Abby longer than anyone at the service. Pierce was much more than Brooks Jenkins' boss. In many ways, Brooks and Abby were family to Bill Pierce and his wife.

Pierce spoke first to Abby and her son, thanking them for years of sacrificing time away from a loving husband and father, allowing Brooks to serve his community. He spoke to the 40 plus officers in uniform sitting together at the back of the church, and to the detectives, telling them how lucky they were to have served alongside Detective Jenkins and to have him as an example to follow. And finally, he addressed the citizens of Stonefield, letting them know how much Jenkins loved representing the Stonefield Police Department and making his hometown a safer place to live.

"There wasn't anything he wouldn't do for this community," Pierce said, his voice cracking for the first time.

As Pierce stepped down from the podium, the organ music resumed, signaling it was time for the pallbearers to return the casket down the aisle to the waiting hearse.

Kerry extended his arm to assist his mother as first to fall in line behind the casket. Angela, along with a dozen of Abby's closest friends, then followed.

A glossy black limo to transport the pallbearers and a dozen gold and black squad cars were lined up before the hearse at the front of the church. The hearse driver waited for the police officers to reach their patrol cars before slowly pulling from the curb and following them to Prairie Rest Cemetery on the edge of town.

With lights flashing and sirens silent, the patrol cars led the hearse to the final resting place of Brooks Jenkins. Citizens of Stonefield lined the sidewalks and streets as the funeral procession slowly passed. Caps were removed and hands placed over hearts in honor of the fallen detective.

In her car among those following the hearse, Angela studied the somber faces of those alongside the road. It was like nothing she'd ever experienced.

The graveside service was short, attended only by the officers and detectives of SPD and Abby's closest friends. After Reverend Miller completed his ceremony, Kerry pulled a rose from the blanket atop the casket and handed it to his mother. Abby sobbed as she held the flower.

Everyone slowly disbursed, and Jack walked silently with Angela to her car.

"His life obviously touched many people," Angela told Jack once inside.

"I was serving overseas and missed my dad's service," Jack replied. "But I was told the turnout for his funeral was similar. I think it's something you only find in smaller communities."

"It's a shame you couldn't get back," she said.

"Pierce is hosting a lunch reception at the VFW hall," Jack said. "Let's stop by for a moment and pay our respects to Abby."

"It's gonna be hard to go back to work today," Angela replied.

"Like Abby pointed out earlier, Jenkins would want us to carry on. We need to solve this murder for him, if for no other reason."

- 12.1 -

JERALD JEFFERSON'S office phone rang. The Cap INC executive recognized the caller ID and picked up.

"What do you want?" Jefferson barked, leaning back in his leather office chair.

"I'm hearing the cops are closing in on our plan to enhance the MedEX pain med," a deep voice replied.

"Our plan? That's a laugh," Jefferson said. "You've played no role in the development of these drugs."

"You're forgetting that if it wasn't for me, MedEX would've been shut down by now, and you and your billionaire boss would be in the middle of a federal investigation," the man argued.

"I think you're taking a little more credit than you deserve," Jefferson said. "I'd never let things get that out of control."

"I still have Sarah Elliott's briefcase, and she kept some very interesting notes on Motts. If any of that information became known, you'd be behind bars."

Jefferson jumped to his feet and yanked his tie loose.

"If you're attempting to blackmail me, that would be the last mistake you'll ever make," he threatened.

"I'm not looking for more money," the man replied. "You compensate me well for my services."

"Then why are you calling?" Jefferson asked, still simmering.

"You were able to get to Motts in prison and make it look like a suicide," the caller replied. "I need the same thing to happen to Rand Elliott, only with one additional requirement."

"What's that?"

"He needs to leave behind a suicide note, saying how sorry he was for killing his wife."

Jefferson dropped back into his chair and rotated to stare out the window.

"You must think I'm some kinda magician."

"I know your capabilities," the caller replied.

"And why do you think killing Rand Elliott is something I'm responsible for doing?"

"Elliott's alibi is gaining support, and if he goes free, the investigation into his wife's murder is going to get ugly—for me and for you," the caller replied. "Cap INC has the money and the connections to get to Elliott. I don't."

There was silence as Jefferson considered the caller's proposal.

"If I'm willing to take on this task you're requesting, I'll need something in return," he finally replied.

"Name it."

"There are two detectives making life difficult at MedEX. I understand they were back again yesterday, pushing around the site manager and one of our security guards."

"What do you want me to do?"

"I want them both taken care of, and I want it to look like an unfortunate accident," Jefferson replied. "I have a plan, but you need to carry it out."

"You've got guys to handle stuff like this. Why me?"

"Because I want your skin in the game. If you screw up, you'll be going down with me!" Jefferson warned. "I'll call later to discuss the details."

- 12.2 -

IT WAS TOO SOON after the funeral and too nice a day to drive to Stonefield Estates to investigate a murder. Yet, that's what Detectives Jones and Fowler had to do.

There was little activity behind the stone pillars guarding the entrance to the upscale community. People were at work. The golf course was slowing down as winter approached. And the murder investigation continued to weigh heavily on the residents, keeping them inside.

Fowler didn't call ahead to warn the Feltons of their visit. He didn't want to give Dr. Felton advance warning, allowing him time to put on a game face.

The garage door was closed and no cars were parked in the driveway as Fowler's oversized cruiser pulled to the curb.

"It doesn't look like anyone's home," Jones said.

"Let's go see."

The two detectives walked briskly up the sidewalk, dressed in slacks and sport coats. Fowler pressed the doorbell and chimes rang inside the sprawling ranch home. Seconds later, Joan Felton appeared wearing jeans and a burnt orange sweater, hair perfectly coiffed. Her eyes widened when she saw the detectives.

"Detective Fowler, I'm surprised to see you," she said pulling the door fully open. "Wasn't your partner's funeral today?"

"Yes. This morning," he replied.

"Several folks from out here attended," Felton said. "I would've gone, but my husband is out of town, and I don't do well at those things by myself."

"Is he home now?" Fowler asked.

"No, he just called from the Dallas airport. He won't get back until later tonight," she replied. "Say, is this the young woman who solved those gruesome murders with you last year?"

Joan Felton studied the female detective.

"I'm Detective Jones, and I'm working this case with Detective Fowler."

"So, you two are back together. That's great."

"Mrs. Felton, we came to ask you and your husband questions about this case," Fowler said. "What time do you expect him to be home?"

"It will be late. His plane lands in Greensboro at six-thirty."

"So around eight or so?"

"Yes. That sounds about right."

Fowler paused, realizing the element of surprise was gone.

"Would it be possible for us to come back then?" he asked. "It shouldn't take more than fifteen minutes."

"Isn't this something you could do over the phone?"

"No, ma'am. We prefer to meet in person with you and Dr. Felton on this," he replied.

"Sounds serious," she said, puckering her face. "We've already told you everything we know."

"We really can't say any more until we meet with both of you. So, is it okay to come back at eight?"

"I guess so. It doesn't sound like we have an option," she replied, slowly closing the door.

"Well, that didn't go very well," Jones said.

"I probably should've called," Fowler replied. "But it doesn't matter now. Felton will have time to get his story together."

- 12.3 -

IT MAY HAVE BEEN a beautiful sunny day outside the Stonefield Jail, but every day inside the eight by ten cell was gloomy and grey for Rand Elliott, now known to his friends and the community as an accused murderer. Eldon Watkins had just arrived to inform his client of the pending statements from the Johnsons.

"You gotta get me outta here now!" Rand Elliott screamed as Watkins entered his cell.

"Can't you go to the DA with this new information and get the charges dropped?" Rand pleaded, pacing his cell like a caged shelter dog.

"I spoke with the DA, and he won't consider dropping the charges or even lowering your bond until he sees the statements from the Johnsons," Watkins replied. "And he said, even then, he needs to consider the total evidence against you."

"Total evidence? What total evidence?" Elliott called out. "I've been framed. I've told you that from the beginning."

"Just give me a few more days," Watkins said. "Once I get the signed statements, I'll go over Ron Olsen's head if I have to and take your case to the district judge."

"I may be dead in a few more days," Elliott moaned. "You saw what happened to my wife's client in Asheville—that Motts fella."

"He was a known drug dealer," Watkins said. "It's hard to tell how he died."

"Somebody got to him. Someone poisoned him!" Elliott wailed, his eyes bulging in fear. "I'm afraid to eat anything in here."

"You need to relax, Elliott. You're gonna have a stroke," Watkins warned. "This is a small-town jail. The jailer's worked here for years. He picks up your meals from Zellar's Café down the street and delivers the food directly to you."

"I won't eat or drink anything that isn't packaged and sealed," Elliott insisted.

"Then you're gonna waste away to nothing," Watkins said. "You're already starting to look like a malnourished street beggar."

"At least I'm alive," he said, taking a seat on his cot.

Elliott leaned forward, elbows on his knees, wringing his hands.

"Can't you fly to Costa Rica and get their statements?" he asked desperately. "Or press Dr. Felton to admit it was me who passed them that night?"

"Going there would only save a day or two by the time I book flights, fly there, and return."

"What's the deal with Felton?" Elliott asked. "He knows damn well it was my car he saw."

"I can't force him to change his mind, but maybe he'll reconsider once he learns of the Johnsons' statements."

Elliott became quiet, staring down at the cement floor.

"Have you learned any more about my wife's side business?" he asked. "Any chance what you heard was wrong?"

"I'm afraid not," Watkins replied.

"You know I cried myself to sleep for several nights," Elliott said, continuing to look down. "I was unable to bear the thought of what she must've experienced in her final moments. I went back and forth between despair and hate for whoever killed her. Now, after learning what she'd been doing, I don't know what to think."

"I wish I could say something that would explain what's happened, but I can't," Watkins replied. "Sometimes people just snap, and we don't know why."

- 12.4 -

FOWLER AND JONES returned to the Feltons' home exactly at 8:00 o'clock. Joan Felton answered the door, dressed in the same clothes as earlier, but appeared drawn. Her eyes were slightly swollen and red.

"Is now a good time?" Jones asked.

"Yeah. Please come into the living room and have a seat," she replied. "Stan is back in his office. He got a call a few minutes ago, but he knows you were coming."

"Have you discussed the Johnsons' statement with your husband?" Jones asked, taking a seat in a chair next to Fowler.

Joan Felton glanced over her shoulder, listening for her husband.

"He's a stubborn man," she said softly. "He rarely admits he's wrong about anything. But I told him the Johnsons are good churchgoing people. They wouldn't lie about something like this."

"And how did he respond?" Fowler asked.

The sound of a door closing was followed by heavy footsteps coming up the hallway. Joan Felton turned to see her husband enter the room as Jones and Fowler rose.

"Stan, you know Detective Fowler," Joan said. "And this is Detective Jones from Charlotte."

Felton stood poker-faced, dressed in slacks and a dress shirt with the top button undone. Appearing slightly nervous, he immediately pulled on the right shirtsleeve with his left hand, shuffling his weight from side to side.

"Please have a seat," he said. "Sorry I had to take that call, but after being away for several days, things mount up."

"I'm sure," Jones said.

Dr. Felton took a seat next to his wife on the sofa as Jones and Fowler lowered into their chairs.

"I understand this is your second visit here today," Felton said, his eyes focusing on Jones. "Whatever you've come to tell me must be important."

"Our main reason for being here is to ask if you've reconsidered what you saw the night of Sarah Elliott's murder," Fowler said. "Are you still sure it wasn't Rand Elliott's car you saw pass the clubhouse that night?"

Dr. Felton glanced at his wife. She looked away.

"I guess it's possible it was Rand's car," he replied. "But I don't recall seeing the Tesla symbol on the hood. Maybe I just missed it."

"So, you're willing to say that it could've been Rand Elliott's car?" Jones asked.

"Yeah. That's what I just said," he replied abruptly.

"You were positive that it *wasn't* his car when we spoke before," Fowler said. "Changing your statement impacts Rand Elliott's alibi and is important to this case. Is there any chance you'll change it again?"

"What's so hard for you to understand?" Felton asked tersely. "I just told you I'm not sure. I hear the Johnsons are willing to be more definitive. You have what you need, so if you don't mind, I have work to do tonight."

Felton stood.

"Joan will see you to the door," he said, taking a step toward the hallway.

"One more question, Dr. Felton," Fowler said. "When was the last time you were at the Vista View Inn in Asheville?"

Felton froze, slowly turning back to Fowler, appearing more puzzled than angry.

"What the hell does that have to do with anything?" he asked.

"Just answer the question," Fowler replied.

Felton looked down at his wife, still seated on the sofa.

"Joan and I stayed there last fall," he said. "We got away for her birthday."

Fowler turned to Jones. She shook her head, warning Fowler not to go any further.

"That's all," he said to Felton.

"You can't just drop a question like that out of thin air!" Felton shouted. "I deserve an explanation. What were you implying?"

"I really can't discuss the case," Fowler said. "You've answered the question."

Felton stared at Fowler for a long moment before turning and stomping down the hall toward his office.

"I apologize for Stan's behavior," Joan said softly. "He hasn't been himself lately. I guess his work schedule is weighing on him, and everyone out here is still on edge about what happened to Sarah."

"Dr. Felton's an orthopedic surgeon. Is that right?" Jones asked.

"Yes. He had a big speech at a conference at the Dallas Omni this past weekend," she replied. "I have a feeling it didn't go well. He was upset the minute he walked in the door tonight."

"What was his speech about?" Jones asked.

"He doesn't tell me much, but I think it had something to do with pain management," she replied. "He consults on that subject. A lot of his patients suffer from joint and back pain."

Jones and Fowler glanced at each other.

"Thanks for your time," Jones said, stepping to the front door. "I hope the rest of your week improves."

"WHAT'S YOUR READ?" Jones asked once inside Fowler's car.

"My first impression is Felton is a bigger ass than I originally had him pegged to be," Fowler replied. "But being an ass isn't against the law."

"Do you think he's been telling the truth about not recognizing Elliott's car?"

"I'm not sure," Fowler replied. "Although, it's possible he didn't see the hood ornament."

"What about his reaction to staying at the Vista View Inn?"

"That one puzzles me," Fowler said. "If he *was* there with Sarah Elliott, why would he challenge me on why I asked the question? He'd given an acceptable answer. Why not let it drop there?"

"Maybe that isn't him in the video," Jones said.

"Or he's smarter than we think. Maybe he didn't expect I'd ask about him being with Sarah in front of his wife."

"And he was right," Jones said.

"He was clearly nervous when he stepped into the living room. He fidgeted with his shirtsleeve a couple times. His mannerisms are very similar to the video, but after seeing him again, his physical features seem different. He's heavier and greyer."

"I wonder what kinda consulting he does on pain management," Jones said.

"I picked up on that, too," Fowler replied. "I think I'll make a call to the Dallas Omni and see what I can find out about the conference."

- Day 13 -
Wednesday

JONES' PHONE CHIRPED on the top of Fowler's dresser. She lifted her head from the pillow and squinted at the clock on the nightstand. It was 7:15.

She sat, slid her feet to the floor, and shuffled toward the phone, picking it up on the fifth ring. It was Lt. Alvarez.

"Good morning, Lieutenant," she said, trying to sound awake.

"I hope I didn't wake you," he said.

"No, sir. I've already had my coffee."

Fowler heard the lie and chuckled. Jones shushed him, putting a finger to her lips.

"If you want this subpoena served on James Statler anytime soon, you're gonna need to help push it through," he said. "There are more questions coming out of the judge's chamber than I can answer."

"Like what?" she asked.

"For one, his law clerk is asking for a specific office address for Statler," he replied. "This clerk also wants evidence of Statler's alleged involvement in the deaths of Motts and Ratcliff."

"You think I need to drive over there?"

"Only if you want to make sure it gets done."

"Alright. I'll get to the courthouse this morning," she said.

"Let me know how it goes."

Fowler sat up in bed.

"Sounds like you're headed back to Charlotte."

"I need to convince Judge Bailey's law clerk of the need to get this subpoena issued," she replied. "Probably not a two-person job. I'll let you know if I have any problems."

"Okay. I wasn't able to find out much about the Dallas medical conference last night," he said. "Maybe I can make progress today during business hours."

"I should get back and check on my place anyway," Jones said. "I'll probably stay the night."

"What's with your boss calling so early?" Fowler asked, puckering his face. "Doesn't he know he's waking me up, too?"

Jones smiled. "I don't think he likes you."

"What's not to like?"

"He's afraid you're trying to steal me away from his department."

"He's right."

"I'd better run," she said. "I'll shower and then grab something to eat on my way."

- 13.1 -

"I'M TERRI SUNDAY, and I was the Omni coordinator for the Orthopedic Medical Professionals Conference held here," the young woman explained. "I received a message from a Detective Fowler requesting a callback."

It was mid-morning and Fowler had been trying to find someone at the Dallas hotel familiar with Dr. Felton's participation at the event.

"Yes. I'm Jack Fowler," he replied. "I called to see if I could get a copy of the conference agenda and possibly a copy of the presentations."

"May I ask what this is for?"

"It's for a criminal investigation, but I really can't say much more than that."

Brief silence.

"I worked with Dr. Jacob Reynolds here in Dallas on the conference," she replied. "He's on the board of the Southwest Orthopedic Medical Association and coordinated the speakers. I'm sure he has copies of all the presentations."

"Could you give me his number?"

"I guess so," she replied before reading the number to him. "Is that all you need?"

"Who attended the conference?" Fowler asked.

"They were orthopedic doctors and health care professionals from across the south—around five hundred in total."

"Any pharmaceutical companies represented?"

"Not that I'm aware of."

"That's all I need for now. Thanks for your help."

NOT WANTING TO DRAW attention to Stan Felton, Fowler called and asked Dr. Reynolds to forward all of the conference presentations to him. Minutes later, he received 22 pdf files sent to his email. Each presentation was more than a dozen pages in length.

He sat at the computer in his den, flipping through color charts, stopping after scanning the first few pages of each presentation and then moving to the next.

Fowler couldn't pronounce most of the titles, let alone understand the medical jargon on the individual charts. Many of the speakers focused on treatments of specific joint injuries resulting from accidents or prolonged wear and tear. Others spoke on new innovations in physical therapy.

Finally, he reached Felton's speech, titled, *Opioids – The Good, Bad, and Ugly in Managing Pain.*

Many of the charts in his presentation illustrated the risks of prescription pain medication, highlighting the dramatic national increase in deaths from overdoses of these drugs. To confront this tragic trend, Felton noted when to prescribe and when not to prescribe opioid painkillers. On the surface, it appeared to be a balanced look at the risks and benefits.

That balance shifted toward the end of his pitch. The presentation closed with charts on the effective utilization of opioids to manage and control pain. Felton even went so far as to highlight several pharmaceutical manufacturers and brands.

Fowler's eyes sprang open when he flipped to a chart dedicated to MedEX. Felton stated the company and its products had a track record of quality, safety, and efficacy. He noted several new features of MedEX medications, such as time-released pain management. As a tease of what was to come, Felton boasted of MedEX's innovative treatments still in development.

Fowler turned off his computer and leaned back.

This connection to MedEX can't be a coincidence, he thought.

He called Jones.

"What's up?" she asked. "I'm still fifteen minutes from the courthouse."

"I found Dr. Felton's speech on pain management," he replied. "He has a chart where he pitches the benefits of MedEX medications. It could be a TV ad for the company."

"Do you think he's getting kickbacks?"

"Anything's possible. He also mentions other drug companies in his presentation, but MedEX clearly stands out," Fowler replied.

"It would be good to know who his contact is at MedEX," Jones said.

"That might be difficult to find out."

"We could obviously ask James Statler if I can make progress on this subpoena," she said. "And speaking of that, could you do me a favor?"

"Name it."

"I'm gonna need Statler's office address. You have Wilson's number at MedEX that he wrote on your card. Could you call him and get his boss's address?"

"I'll call right now."

WILSON'S OFFICE PHONE rang several times before he picked up.

"Wilson here."

"This is Detective Fowler. I need your CEO's office address."

"What for?"

"We need to know where to serve the investigative subpoena," Fowler replied, "so we can go question him."

"He's rarely there," Wilson nervously lied.

"Doesn't matter. Give me the address, including floor and office number."

Wilson's forehead glistened with sweat. He knew providing the address could be his final act at MedEX.

"How soon do you expect to be delivering this subpoena?" Wilson asked.

"Hard to tell. Possibly as early as tomorrow if everything moves quickly."

Wilson stared at the box of documents in the corner of his office that he'd been packing that morning.

"So, it won't be served today?"

"Tomorrow at the earliest. Now tell me his address."

"He's at 125 Business Park Road, Charlotte, Suite 501, 5th floor."

A knock came to Wilson's office door.

"I need to go," he told Fowler. "Someone's here."

A bearded dock foreman dressed in jeans and a logoed denim work shirt entered the office.

"Mr. Wilson, we have trucks arriving today to load the new pain med. Is it okay to start shipping it out?"

"You can begin loading, but hold off on shipping until Mr. Statler gets back to you," Wilson replied.

The man looked puzzled.

"Mr. Statler?"

"That's right."

"Okay. I'll let everyone know."

The dock foreman left, and Wilson resumed packing.

- 13.2 -

IT HAD BEEN A LONG DAY at the Mecklenburg County Courthouse for Detective Jones, most of it spent waiting for Judge Bailey's law clerk and the county's administrative staff to meet with her. It was late afternoon before she headed to the SBI district office to update Lt. Alvarez.

"I hope Statler cooperates after he's served with the subpoena," Jones told Alvarez. "I hate to think I wasted a full day pushing paper through the system for nothing."

"So, Judge Bailey is going to sign off?"

"It looks that way," she replied. "I even went to the DA's office to alert him we were paying a call on the MedEX CEO, and of possible charges coming down."

"Charges? You seem to be putting a lot of hope in Statler's testimony. Don't you think that's a little optimistic?"

"There's something rotten going on at his company. He can't hide it much longer," she replied.

"How's the Elliott murder investigation going in Stonefield?"

"Fowler and I met with Dr. Felton last night. He wasn't real cooperative, but he did say that he may've been wrong about the car not belonging to Rand Elliott. And it's still not clear what, if any, connection he had with Sarah Elliott."

"So, he's no longer a person of interest?"

"Not necessarily," she replied. "Based on a presentation Fowler discovered, Dr. Felton might have a cozy relationship with MedEX promoting the company's pain meds."

"You keep uncovering more puzzle pieces. They'd better start fitting together soon," Alvarez replied.

"It's been a long road so far, but I think we're near the end."

"Let me know if you need help with anything else," he said. "Otherwise, I'm going to assume you and Fowler are running with this."

"That's fine," she replied. "I'll be heading home in a few minutes. We'll talk tomorrow."

JONES CALLED FOWLER on the way to her house to let him know they might be able to get to Statler as early as tomorrow. They agreed to touch base first thing in the morning.

Her home was dark as she pulled into the driveway with only the porch lights illuminated. It had been several days since she'd been home, and she looked forward to soaking in her own garden tub. She hit the button to raise the garage door, pulled her blue Volvo inside, and then lowered the door behind her.

The house was quiet with everything as she'd left it. Jones went to the kitchen and pulled down a wineglass from the cabinet beside the refrigerator. She uncorked a bottle of Chardonnay and filled the glass with a generous pour. Before heading to the living room, she removed her jacket and holster and hung them on a wall peg.

As she reached for the hall light switch, a deep voice came from the darkness of the living room.

"Freeze right where you are!" a man shouted.

Startled, she dropped the wineglass. It shattered on the wood floor, propelling shards of glass and wine down the hallway.

In the shadows, a man rose from her reading chair in the living room. Dressed in a black sweatshirt and dark pants, his arm was extended with a .45 caliber handgun pointed at her.

She didn't recognize him in the darkness. He slowly stepped from the shadows and into the light filtering from the kitchen. It was Dr. Stan Felton.

"Very careless of you using your badge number as your security code," he said. "You'd think a detective would be more cautious."

"What do you want?" she asked, showing no fear.

"You get right to the point, don't you, detective? I'm here to do a little housekeeping. You and Detective Fowler have become a problem for me and my partners."

"Whatever you've planned, you'll never pull it off," she said boldly. "Too many people are onto you."

"Not that many," he argued. "Not even you and Fowler have figured me out yet. Have you?"

"It seems clear now," she said. "Why did you kill Sarah Elliott?"

"Clever. Are you looking for me to confess?" he asked with an evil grin. "That's fine with me. It won't do you much good after tonight."

"What did she do to deserve being stabbed to death?" Jones asked, hoping he'd tell all.

"She profited from my work with MedEX but decided to throw it all away, and I couldn't have her do that," he replied.

"Throw it away? How?"

"She was going to blow the whistle on me, MedEX, and our plans. She was fine with the substantial payment for representing Motts, but when she learned what MedEX was up to, she couldn't let people die."

"Who's gonna die? What people?"

"It doesn't matter," he said, extending the weapon. "I gave her a chance to change her mind. I even offered to pay for one more night with her, but she spit in my face, told me to leave, and then ran into the bathroom. I found a knife in the kitchen, wrapped it in a towel, and waited for her to come out. The next thing I remember, she was dead on the floor."

"What is MedEX up to?" she asked. "Who's gonna die?"

"Forget about it. Knowing won't do you any good."

"Do you really think you'll get away with this?" she asked.

"I already have," he sneered. "By the time I leave here, Rand Elliott will have left a letter of confession and be dead in his cell."

Keeping the gun pointed at Jones, he picked up a bag near the chair where he'd been sitting. He reached inside, removed a roll of silver duct tape, and stepped toward Jones.

"Get back in the kitchen and take a seat in that chair," he said, pointing to a wooden ladder-back chair beside the table.

She stepped to the chair and sat.

"Put your hands behind your back!" he ordered.

Keeping the gun in his hand, he pulled a long strip of tape from the roll with his teeth and used it to secure Jones' wrists. He then wound the roll around and around her wrists several times before ripping it off. Finally, he secured each of her ankles to the front legs of the chair.

"Where's your cellphone?" he asked.

"I left it at the office."

"Don't bullshit me!" he shouted, slapping her face with the back of his hand. "Where is it?"

"It's in my jacket over there," she said, pointing with her head.

He rummaged through the pockets and pulled out the phone.

"Give me your security code!" he demanded.

"Go screw yourself."

Felton reared his arm back, slapping the other side of Jones' face, ripping the corner of her mouth.

Jones closed her eyes and shook her head as blood dripped down her chin. The room was spinning when she looked up at Felton standing over her.

"I'll give you one more chance to tell me the code," he said.

"You can beat me all you want, but I'm not telling."

He set his gun on the kitchen counter and pecked at the phone's security keypad. The phone unlocked.

"You must use your badge number for everything," he said, grinning.

"What are you doing?"

"I need to get your boyfriend over here," he replied. "The two of you are going to experience a tragic accident tonight. Gas leaks can be very deadly."

Jones' eyes widened.

"How does this text to Detective Fowler sound?" he asked. *"Jack, I'm sick. Food poisoning? Could you come tonight? If I don't answer, I'm in the bathroom."*

Felton hit enter. A minute later, Fowler replied.

Hang on. Be there in an hour.

"That should leave me plenty of time to finish setting up my little trap," he said, setting the phone on the counter.

"What trap?"

"I've wired your security entry pads to an electrical switch that will initiate a spark exactly seven seconds after your code is entered."

"Why seven seconds?" she asked.

A demented grin spread to his face.

"I want to make sure Fowler is well inside before the spark ignites a blast that will be heard in uptown Charlotte," he replied. "There'll be no need to cremate your bodies. I'll save everyone the trouble and expense."

"You're a sick man," she growled.

"A very *rich* sick man," he replied, "who will soon be departing to safer and warmer surroundings."

She tugged at the bindings on her wrists. They didn't budge.

"You're not going anywhere, Detective," he said. "Now if you don't mind, I have some final preparations before I meet my driver down the street."

He stuffed a paper towel in Jones' mouth and secured it by wrapping duct tape around her head.

Felton hurried to the garage and enabled the electrical switch connected to the entry keypad. He then loosened the gas valve to the nearby water heater before returning to the kitchen. After pulling the oven from the wall, he loosened the gas valve near the floor. A low hiss could be heard.

"The gas may get to you before the blast," Felton said. "Either way, it should be painless."

Before leaving, he stuffed Jones' cellphone into his pocket and pulled the cords to the house phones from the walls.

Jones yanked and pulled her hands, but the tape held firm. The bindings around her legs were as tight as tourniquets. Her feet were numb from lack of blood flow.

Jones noticed the microwave clock read 7:45 when Felton sent the text to Fowler. Fifteen minutes had already elapsed, not leaving much time to escape from her bindings.

She tried to use her toes to scoot the chair, but her feet were bound above the floor. By rocking her weight from side to side while leaning forward, she was able to move the chair forward by fractions of an inch with each rock.

She looked around the kitchen for something she could scrape against the tape that was binding her hands. There were no sharp edges at the same height of her bound wrists. The doorframe was a possibility, but it was painted wood. It would take forever for the dull edge of the frame to wear away the tape. Still, it was all she could see.

She began rocking and leaning toward the doorway. It was a tiring, slow process, pulling at her stomach muscles. She paused several times to catch her breath.

Natural gas was beginning to fill the room. The putrid smell of rotten eggs stung her nose and fogged her head. Jones knew natural gas was lighter than air and would fill the ceiling space before eventually engulfing the entire room. With 35 minutes remaining, she rocked more quickly, but was still only halfway to the doorframe.

Exhausted, she finally reached the door. She rocked and twisted the chair to get her back against the frame. There were only 15 minutes before Fowler would arrive.

I pray he's running late, she thought.

Jones began scraping the tape against the edge of the frame, only able to move her wrists an inch or two with each pass. Her shoulders ached as she forced her wrists against the frame at an awkward angle.

Just five minutes remained.

Knowing I'm sick, he's probably speeding. He could be here any minute.

The smell of the gas was much stronger. Feeling dizzy, she closed her eyes to think. She tested the tape one more time. It held tight. There was no sign of progress.

I have to try something else.

Jones recalled replacing broken spindles in the ladder-back chairs in years past. Falling to the floor to break the chair might work, but she knew it would be her final option.

If this fails, it's been a good ride.

She rocked violently, intending to fall with the back of the chair hitting against the doorframe. On the third attempt, the chair toppled backwards and crashed to the floor. She tested her hands and feet. They were still secured to the chair.

Lying sideways on the floor, Jones was able to kick with her legs, beating the chair against the doorway. She frantically tried again and again to free her legs. Finally, the right chair leg made a loud crack. Jones continued ramming the chair against the door until the chair leg splintered and her right ankle came free.

Unable to stand on one freed leg, she resumed beating the other chair leg against the doorframe, but it was holding firm.

She paused to catch her breath as headlights flashed through the front windows of her home and across the ceiling.

Desperately, she smashed the chair leg against the door like a woman possessed by demons. The wooden leg finally broke loose and she was able to stand. Her arms were still secured behind her back to what remained of the chair.

She heard the engine of Fowler's car shut off and his door slam as she backed to a drawer filled with kitchen utensils. She rummaged through the drawer, feeling for a knife. It took her just a few seconds to maneuver the knife upward and cut her wrists free.

With the tape still around her head and mouth, she heard the garage door going up and ran out the front door.

Seven, six, five, she counted inside her head as she ran. With seconds remaining, Fowler turned to see Jones sprinting toward him.

She hit Fowler waist high like a 230-pound defensive back flattening a punt returner. The force propelled both of them across the driveway and down a ravine beside the neighbor's home. She pulled him low in the ravine just as the world seemed to disintegrate above them.

The explosion sent a fireball 200 feet skyward, illuminating an area two miles in every direction. The concussion from the blast shattered windows of homes several doors away. Lying flat against the ground, flaming debris fell around them like fallout from an apocalyptic storm.

Moments later, with the danger finally passed, Fowler sat and helped Jones remove the tape from around her head. A loud ringing in their ears drowned out all other sounds.

"What happened?" he mouthed.

Jones pulled the paper towel from her mouth and yelled, "It was Dr. Felton!"

Jones attempted to stand, but quickly fell back to the ground. With all the adrenalin flowing through her body, she hadn't felt the gaping wound on her lower right leg. Fowler tossed his sport coat aside and removed his white shirt. After tearing it into strips, he wrapped the 6-inch gash on her leg to subdue the bleeding.

"EMTs will be here soon," he said before helping her to the sidewalk across the street.

"You need to warn Pierce," she groaned. "Rand Elliott is in danger."

"What?" Fowler yelled.

"Rand Elliott!" she shouted. "They're gonna kill him!"

- 13.3 -

FIRST RESPONDERS arrived at the scene of the widespread devastation in a matter of minutes. Debris was scattered 100 yards in all directions. No walls of the home were left standing. A bathtub and commode were in the yard next door, and a stone planter box that once set beside the front door had been rocketed across the street into the side of an SUV.

Other than a few scrapes and cuts from the tumble down the ravine, Fowler had survived the explosion in good condition. But the gash to Jones' leg needed attention.

With the fire department tending to the smoldering remains of what had been Detective Jones' home, a paramedic wearing a white jacket jumped from the passenger side of an arriving ambulance and went directly to Jones. He quickly assessed her injury.

"This will require stitches," the young medic said. "We'll need to get you to the hospital."

"For this little cut? I don't need to go to the hospital for this," she objected. "Can't *you* put in a couple of stitches?"

"I can clean and wrap it and give you something for the pain, but I'm not authorized to treat a wound like this."

"Well, I'm not leaving here just for this. That was my house over there."

"Maybe you should listen to him," Fowler said. "You don't want to deal with an infection later."

Jones thought as the paramedic tended to her leg.

"Can an RN stitch me up?" she asked.

"Sure, but we don't have an RN on this ambulance."

"My neighbor two doors down in that white house is an RN," Jones said, pointing down the street. "Have your partner go see if Roxanne Smith is home. She's a tall brunette."

The paramedic glanced at the dark-haired EMT standing near the rear of the ambulance.

"I'll see what I can do," he said, before running toward the white house.

The ringing Jones' ears was slowly subsiding, and he was finally able to call Stonefield PD. After leaving a message for Pierce, he was transferred to Officer Sillar, the officer on duty.

"Get a couple of squad cars out to Stonefield Estates and arrest Dr. Stan Felton. Consider him armed and dangerous," Fowler yelled over the roar of the fire trucks. "Felton confessed to killing Sarah Elliott. I'll explain the rest later."

"I'll get right on it. Anything else?" Sillar asked.

"There's a death threat against Rand Elliott. Put an armed guard outside his cell now!" he shouted.

"What kind of threat?" Sillar asked.

"I don't have details on how or when, but make sure a guard oversees Elliott's food preparation."

"His dinner was delivered an hour ago," the thick-chested officer replied. "But he never eats it. He's been living on Coke and candy bars."

"Call the jailhouse right now and check on him."

"Will do."

AFTER DISPATCHING two squad cars to Dr. Felton's home in Stonefield Estates, Officer Sillar hurried to the jailhouse and walked with the jailer to Elliott's cell.

Elliott sat on his cot, drinking a can of Coke, his dinner tray untouched on a chair beside him.

"You doing okay?" Sillar asked.

"I'm fine," Elliott sneered. "Why all the attention?"

"No reason. Just checking."

Sillar turned to the jailer.

"Fowler said you need to stand guard outside his cell."

"What?" the jailer whined. "I'll go nuts sitting in here. I have a radio at my desk to pass the time."

"Just do it," Sillar ordered, heading back to his duty station.

Minutes later, still sitting on his cot, Elliott unwrapped a Snickers bar and bit off a third of it. He chewed and swallowed the mouthful of candy. Before he could take another bite, his eyes filled with panic, and he reached for his chest. He turned and dropped his feet to the floor as he sat on the edge of his cot, struggling for breath.

"Something's wrong," he gasped. "I'm gonna pass…"

In mid-sentence, Elliott fell to the cement floor.

The jailer unlocked the cell door and rushed inside. He lowered his ear to Rand's face and listened for breathing. He was alive, but just barely.

The lanky jailer radioed Officer Sillar, telling him that Elliott had passed out. He then began administering CPR to the pale-faced man on the floor. It wasn't working.

By the time Sillar reached the cell, Elliott appeared lifeless, lying faceup, eyes closed. The color had drained from his face and lips.

"Had he eaten anything?"

"Just a candy bar," the jailer replied.

"Is there Narcan in the jailhouse?" Sillar shouted.

"What's that?" the jailer asked, shrugging his shoulders.

"Forget it! Just keep shaking him," Sillar ordered. "Try to get him back."

The officer ran down the aisle toward the police station. He returned less than a minute later with two doses of Narcan. With Elliott showing no signs of life, he injected the first dose into his thigh.

Sillar watched for evidence the injection had worked. After waiting a minute with no response, he injected the second dose.

"This better bring him back," he said. "It's the last dose in the building."

Almost immediately, Elliott's arm began to flinch and then his eyes blinked.

"He's coming around!" Sillar shouted. "Call for an ambulance. I'll stay with him."

Ten minutes later, EMTs loaded Elliott onto a gurney and rolled him down the aisle

Wondering how this could have happened, Officer Sillar began searching the cell. When he lifted the lid on the dinner tray, he noticed a white paper napkin stuck to the bottom. He peeled the napkin from the lid. A message had been printed on it. It read:

> *I'm sorry for all the pain I've caused everyone.*
> *I loved my wife. I don't know why I did it.*

- 13.4 -

THE EMT FOUND Roxanne Smith outside her home surveying the damages from the blast. The tall RN was more than willing to tend to her neighbor. She carefully applied four stitches to the laceration to Jones' leg and provided a two-day supply of pain meds with instructions to get to a doctor before the supply ran out.

Fowler continued to sit with Jones at the back of the ambulance. It had been nearly two hours since Felton fled the Charlotte neighborhood and no one had reported seeing him. The police officers sent to Felton's home found it empty. They sat in silence on a side street, waiting for Felton to turn up.

Officer Sillar notified Fowler of the failed poisoning attempt and that Elliott was in stable condition at Stonefield General.

"Keep a guard on him around the clock," Fowler ordered. "And keep this out of the press for now. We've got enough going on without explaining this."

The pain meds were effectively dulling Jones' pain, but they were also dulling her senses and causing her to slur her speech.

"Don't cha think it'd be good if Felton thinks it worked?" she asked Fowler. "He won't be on da defensive den."

Fowler somehow got her point. If Felton thought his crimes and confessions died with Jones, he'd have no reason to hide.

Given the magnitude of the event, Captain Reggie McDonald of CMPD had come to the site of the explosion to coordinate the response team. Fowler asked a nearby officer if he'd get word to McDonald to stop by the ambulance and meet with him and Jones.

Minutes later, McDonald appeared wearing a white saucer hat with a glossy black bill.

"I'm Detective Fowler and this is Detective Jones. This explosion was meant for us," he told McDonald. "That rubble used to be her home."

"It's a miracle you're alive," McDonald said.

"Detective Jones is a tough egg. She saved us both."

"You called me over. What can I do for you?" the captain asked.

"We think it would be best if the guy who did this thinks he succeeded," Fowler said. "It might make him easier to find."

"Are you suggesting I report your deaths?" McDonald asked. "What about your next of kin? They'll be unnecessarily devastated."

"Oddly, neither of us has close family," Fowler replied. "We're the closest thing to next of kin we have."

"I'd have a hard time falsely reporting two deaths," the captain replied. "How about just stating that the location of the residents is unknown?"

"That should work," Fowler replied. "I'll make sure Stonefield PD and Jones' SBI unit issue the same statement—at least for a day or two."

"Where do you think your attempted killer went?" McDonald asked.

"The guy's name is Dr. Stan Felton. We thought he was headed home to Stonefield, but he hasn't shown up."

"Is there anything else I can do for you?" McDonald asked.

"See that beast of a vehicle under that debris over there?" Fowler said, pointing to the Grey Ghost.

"Yeah. Don't tell me that's your car," he replied with a chuckle.

"If you'd be so kind as to clear these emergency vehicles from the end of the driveway, I'm going to pull the junk from the roof and drive Detective Jones back to Stonefield."

OTHER THAN A FEW dents on the roof and some minor scorched spots on the hood from burning debris, Fowler's Chrysler sedan was mechanically sound.

"Why is my beautiful home and everything I owned destroyed and this hunk of metal is still rolling down the highway?" Jones asked, lying in the back seat.

"We're lucky it survived or we'd be looking for a ride," Fowler replied.

Ten miles south of Stonefield, Fowler's phone buzzed with a text message. He pulled the phone from his pocket and coasted to a stop beside the road. The text read:

I'm headed out of the country. You can find my boss at this address. Get to him soon or thousands will die. Heavy surveillance to the front. Thick forest to the rear. A show of force will fail. J. Wilson.

A Google Maps URL was attached to the text pointing to the home owned by James Statler.

"Who was it?" Jones asked.

"It's a cell number not in my directory, but it's signed by J. Wilson."

"The site manager at MedEX?"

"Yeah. I guess. He attached the address of his boss's residence with a warning similar to the one Rose Ratcliff left you."

Fowler read the entire note to Jones.

"What are you going to do?" she asked.

"I don't know, but if I contact Alvarez or Pierce, they'll opt for a show of force."

"You can't be thinking of going there by yourself."

"I'm Army Special Forces trained. Going alone, I could scope it out without confronting Statler."

"Without confronting him? This from a guy who recently beat up a security guard?" she scoffed. "Confrontation should be your middle name. Face it. You're gonna need help."

"Thousands dying sounds serious," Fowler replied. "According to the text, Pierce and Alvarez could win the battle with a show of force but lose the war. It's not worth the risk."

"I'm of no use to you," she said. "I guess you'll need to go it alone."

"Actually, it's the only way," he replied. "I'll gear up when I get home. This address is near Lake Norman. I should be able to get there before midnight."

- 13.5 -

DRESSED IN BLACK, Fowler was equipped with night vision binoculars and a through-the-wall sound surveillance system slightly larger than a cellphone. He'd acquired the surveillance device from an army buddy who'd been asked to test it. The system was not approved for police use in North Carolina, making any evidence gathered using it inadmissible in court. His mission was surveillance and not apprehension, but he was armed with a .38 caliber handgun and two extra clips just in case.

As anticipated, he arrived near midnight. He parked his car beside a storage shed less than a mile to the southwest of the address he'd been given.

The Google Maps arial view of the massive home showed it centered on five acres and facing Lake Norman. A front yard the size of a football field separated the house from the water. Tall fencing ran down both borders. He anticipated there'd be cameras scanning the front yard and the frontage road that ran along the lake, dead ending at the driveway of the estate.

Jeremy Wilson was right about the forest to the rear being the only way to approach. From the road, there was one way to the home and one way out. Anyone arriving from the front would quickly be detected.

It took less than fifteen minutes to get from his car to the dense woods behind the home. Kneeling in pine needles 100 yards to the rear of the stone and brick-clad structure, he could see lighted rooms on the first and second floors through the binoculars. It not only appeared someone was home, but someone was still awake.

Fowler crept closer, staying in the shadows of the tall pines. He paused and crouched behind a tree, focusing his night vision binoculars on the back of the home.

A deck ran the entire length of the first floor, standing ten feet above the walkout basement. There was only one stairway to access the deck. It was at the far end, with a tall gate blocking entry from the yard.

Scanning left to right on the first floor, he went window to window, searching for movement inside. About halfway across the back of the massive mansion, he saw two figures standing near a wall of sliding glass doors off the deck. At that distance, he could only tell they were men.

He moved closer, to where the woods stopped and the grassy backyard began. He was now less than 30 yards away. Fowler was amazed he was able to get so close to the home without being detected, but then it didn't appear anyone had ever traveled the route he'd taken.

He again sited through the binoculars. He could clearly see the two men, one black and one white. The black man was taller, fit and dressed in jacket and tie. The other man was in a dark sweater and slacks. Neither man faced the window as they drank from glasses.

Fowler was still too far away to deploy the sound surveillance system. He thought about darting across the grass expanse to the base of the home. He could easily listen to conversations from beneath the deck with the aid of the electronic device.

He estimated it would take less than ten seconds to cross the lawn, but in the moonlight, the men might see him. Worse, the dozen unlit floodlights along the eve of the second story might be activated by motion detectors.

Fowler waited until the men moved further inside the home and away from the windows, and then he bolted toward the deck. Halfway across the lawn the floodlights popped on, illuminating the backyard like a night game at Yankee Stadium. Fowler ducked into the shadows under the deck and froze.

Heavy footsteps rushed onto the deck directly above him and moved to the railing. For a moment, the men stood silently as they scanned the yard.

"Probably deer setting it off again," one man said. "It happens nearly every night."

Fowler assumed the voice belonged to James Statler.

"You know it's not bad out here," the second man said. "Hard to believe it's October."

Fowler immediately recognized the second voice. It was Dr. Felton.

"You'd have to agree that it's been a good day all around," Felton said. "I got rid of the two detectives who'd been a pain in your side, and Rand Elliott died in prison, leaving a note saying how sorry he was that he killed his wife."

"The only dull spot in a bright day was my cowardly site manager skipping town," Statler said, "leaving me to authorize tomorrow's shipments of our new med. It should be in pharmacies across the Southeast soon."

"That's great," Felton replied, before tipping back his glass.

"You know what shipping this product means, don't you?" Statler asked, his face solemn.

"That thousands of patients will be even more dependent on your potent painkiller?"

"No, it means I no longer need your services," Statler replied, pulling a handgun from under his jacket.

"Wait a minute, Jefferson. Put the gun down!" Felton shouted. "Let's talk this over."

Jefferson? Who's Jefferson? Fowler wondered.

"MedEX would be nowhere without me opening up distribution, " Felton pleaded.

"You've done your job, and now you're just a loose end," Jefferson said. "And I cut off loose ends."

Fowler pulled his .38 from his holster and jumped far enough into the yard to clearly see the two men above.

"Police! Drop the weapon or I'll shoot!"

Startled, Jefferson wheeled toward Fowler and fired a shot, missing wildly to the left.

Fowler fired off two quick rounds at the dark silhouette above, aiming a pistol at him. The first hit Jefferson in his shoulder, knocking the gun from his hand onto the deck. The second shot hit him in the chest, splitting Jefferson's sternum. He dropped to his knees, eyes bulging. He froze for a brief moment with a look of horror before tumbling facedown onto the deck.

Felton turned and fled toward the house.

"Stop right there!" Fowler shouted. "Put your hands on your head!"

He slid to a halt and turned toward Fowler.

"Walk slowly toward the stairs at that end, and stay next to the railing where I can see you."

Felton did as he was told. They met at the bottom of the stairs where Felton unlocked the gate and stepped out.

"Take off your shoes and give me the laces," Fowler ordered.

Fowler took the laces from Felton and tied his hands behind him before leading him to the front of the home where he called 911.

DR. STAN FELTON was going away for a long time, and he knew it. With the autumn moonlight reflecting off the still lake, Fowler read him his rights. They stood at the end of the driveway, waiting for CMPD to arrive.

"So, where's Statler?" Fowler asked. "I thought this was his place."

"He doesn't exist. MedEX is owned and operated by Cap INC. Jefferson, the guy you killed, ran it. Having MedEX appear privately owned made it easier to keep questionable business activity an arm's length away from Cap INC. They're running other companies set up the same way."

"Who can stop the drug shipments you were discussing out on the deck?" Fowler asked.

"Go to the top, Erik Rolland," Felton replied. "If I'm going to prison, it's only fair he's in the cell next to mine."

Three CMPD vehicles came roaring up the street toward the Lake Norman mansion. The red and blue lights strobing off the lake gave the appearance of fireworks.

The vehicles slid to a stop yards away from Fowler. To his surprise, Captain McDonald was among the six CMPD officers who leapt from the cruisers.

"You get around, don't you, Detective?" he said, stepping toward Fowler.

"This is the man who tried to kill me and Detective Jones earlier tonight," Fowler said, handing Felton over to one of McDonald's officers.

"You're out of your jurisdiction," McDonald said. "You know that, don't you?"

"I'd normally be working this case with Detective Jones from the Charlotte SBI office, but as you saw earlier, she was in no condition to assist in this apprehension."

"Nice try, Detective," he replied. "But I'm gonna have to write you up on this one. Nine-one-one dispatch said someone was killed."

"He fired at me first, and he was about to shoot Dr. Felton before I stopped him."

"You aren't authorized to be making arrests in this county."

"Seriously? You're gonna write me up for apprehending two killers and saving who knows how many patients from deadly meds?" Fowler argued.

"I'll write you up and file the report in my desk. But if you ever pull another Rambo stunt like this in my county, you'll be lucky to get a job as a mall security guard."

They stared at each other for a long moment.

"Can someone take me to my car?" Fowler asked. "It's been a long day."

- Day 14 -

Conclusion

JONES WAS SOUND ASLEEP aided by pain meds. She never heard Fowler enter the bedroom. Her bandaged leg was sticking out from the sheets. Fowler tucked it back under the covers and gave her a kiss on the forehead.

Exhausted, he couldn't sleep. The investigations had taken a toll on both of them. Jones had lost everything she owned, but they were only possessions. They still had each other, and together they'd decide on the best way to move forward.

Their work was their life. They'd both grown up in homes with fathers in law enforcement. The thrill of the hunt was a big factor in what drove them, but being a part of something bigger than themselves was also a major reason they served.

Fowler finally fell asleep, knowing he was in a good place.

JONES WOKE with Fowler beside her. She'd last seen him leaving the house around 11 p.m., driving back to Charlotte to confront James Statler.

Her leg throbbed in pain. She reached for a bottle of pills on the nightstand and washed one down with a drink of water. She was told to take a tablet every six hours. It had been almost ten, but she figured she needed the sleep more than the meds.

Fowler was safe, and for now, that's what mattered. Still, she was dying to find out what had happened.

While she could wait to learn about James Statler and MedEX, she couldn't put off getting to the bathroom. Her crutches were leaning against the wall on the other side of the nightstand.

The meds had already begun to dull the pain in her leg, but they also dulled her senses. She swung her good leg off the edge of the bed first and then the bandaged leg. Jones sat for a moment, waiting for the room to stop spinning before hopping toward the crutches.

After securing one under each arm, she successfully navigated an overdue trip to the bathroom. She then went to the closet to find something to slip on. For a long moment, Angela stared at what remained of her wardrobe.

A couple of blouses and a dark skirt hung at one end of the closet. She elected to slip on an old terry cloth bathrobe before hobbling toward the kitchen.

Minutes later, she sat at the table sipping coffee and staring out at the backyard through a wide kitchen window.

I've got some decisions to make, she thought.

It had been a wild two years since meeting Jack. They had given each other space to do their work and to live their lives, but it was clear they'd become a couple.

I can't live without him, and he sure as hell needs me.

AN HOUR LATER, Fowler shuffled down the hall and into the living room where Jones had her leg elevated on a footstool, drinking her second cup of coffee. He was dressed in a t-shirt and sweatpants with the drawstring draping halfway to the floor. With his thick dark hair askew, he resembled a deserted island castaway.

He walked to Jones and gave her a warm kiss on the lips. She cradled the back of his head, holding him close.

"Was I ever glad to see you this morning," she said.

"How are you feeling?" he asked.

"Better now. Tell me what happened."

"Let me get a cup of coffee first," he said, heading to the kitchen.

He returned and took Jones through the entire adventure as she listened without interruption.

"There's one thing I can't understand. How did Felton get out of the house and kill Sarah without his wife knowing?" Jones asked. "They were to go to dinner with the Elliotts that night."

"Felton confessed to everything after I turned him over to CMPD. It appears he told his wife he was going for a run before dinner. It was already dark when he reached the Elliotts' house and let himself inside."

"What about all the blood? Surely, Felton's wife must've noticed."

"After killing Sarah, Felton removed his shoes to not track blood. He took Sarah's briefcase from the hall closet before leaving, and then he deposited the knife in the garbage can on his way home. His wife was in the bedroom getting ready for dinner when he arrived. Felton bagged his jogging clothes in the garage and showered in a guest bathroom as he often did after an evening run."

"I still can't believe he didn't leave some tracks behind," Jones said.

"Rand Elliott must've unknowingly destroyed whatever evidence Felton left in the bedroom."

"This is too wild even for me to believe," she said. "But it sounds like it's finally over."

"Yeah, other than a ton of paperwork ahead of me," Fowler replied.

"Does Pierce know about all this?"

"I called the officer on duty to report what happened and also left Pierce a voicemail before going to bed. I can't believe he hasn't called me yet. I'll go into the station soon and explain everything."

"I'm sure he'll understand."

"He'll be upset that I didn't tell him I was going back to Charlotte, but he'll get over it," Fowler replied. "The bad guys are either dead or in jail, and an innocent man has been freed."

Jones was quiet, staring at Jack with reflective eyes.

"What is it?" he asked.

"I've been doing a lot of thinking this morning," she began. "Having your house blown up will cause you to assess your life."

"Have you had any revelations?"

"I was struck by the outpouring of support this community gave to Brooks Jenkins and Abby. They clearly valued his service."

"No doubt he'll be missed."

"I've always been proud of the progress I've made as a black woman in our profession. I'd wrongly thought that by moving here, I'd be taking a step backwards. But after getting a better look at Stonefield, I no longer feel that way. In fact, I believe I could have an even bigger impact here."

"Are you saying what I think you're saying?" Jack asked.

"I'm saying I'm ready to take Chief Pierce up on his offer," she replied. "And after I spend some time and money fixing this place up, I'm sure it will seem like home."

Jack leaned down and wrapped Angela in his arms.

"Sounds great, but the Grey Ghost stays."

Please Provide a Review

Please let the author and other readers know what you think of **ROAD TO JUSTICE** by going to Amazon.com and Goodreads.com to provide a rating and review.

Thank You

About the Author

D.R. (Donn) Shoultz hails from a small town in central Illinois, but has called North Carolina home for more than 25 years. Donn writes at his mountain home off the Blue Ridge Parkway where his wife Claudia shares her considerable editing experience in shaping his novels. In their free time, they both enjoy traveling and hiking nearby wooded trails with their dog, Milo.

Donn's recent focus is his *Mountain Mystery Series*. He defines the stories in this series as "Cozy Mysteries with a Bite." Each book stands on its own, featuring unsolved murders haunting peaceful mountain communities. Hometown heroes step forward to seek justice, often falling into the path of the killers. You'll find crisp, fast-moving chapters, page-turning suspense, and supporting casts you'll long remember. Look for your favorite heroes to appear in future novels.

In his *Miles Stevens Series,* a time-traveling CIA agent travels back from his 2050 Langley, Virginia office to halt epic disasters already in the history books. With terrorist attacks occurring in the 2020s, Miles and his team race against time to save thousands of lives.

You can learn more about D.R. Shoultz and his writing at http://DRShoultz.com

Made in the USA
Columbia, SC
28 February 2022

56566932R00159